BEOWUFF
AND THE
HOrrid HEN

TRANSLATION BY
BURNS-LONGSHIP

BEOWUFF AND THE HORRID HEN

First published by Mogzilla in 2011

Paperback edition:
ISBN: 9781906132385

Text copyright © 2011 Robin Price and Richard Eccles.
Cover illustration by Chris Watson © 2011.
Concept © Mogzilla 2010.

www.mogzilla.co.uk

Printed in the UK

Thanks to: Michele, Richard, Carole, Scarlet, Chris and Luke.

PROLOGUE

The fire is lit in the hall and wood smoke rises from the pit. You and your bench-mates are gathered, with bowls of meat-mead and bones a plenty, ready to see out the night.

So here comes my story. I've promised you a real 'Head-Saver,' a tale that will keep my neck from your Sea King's axe, and I've sworn to leave not a single word out.

Your cruel Lord has made me a promise. He says he'll cut me off in mid-sentence and make a blood-stump of my collar if he sniffs the smallest whiff of a lie from me.

So I promise to tell the whole tale true for once, even if it makes poor Beowuff look less of a lord-dog than you'll find in the other sagas.

Beowuff's tale begins on the whale-road. Now, as every pup knows, the 'whale-road' means the sea – a road for the whale fish and all his fishy kin.

Beowuff is me, by the way, in case the weak-wits amongst you were wondering. So sup up your meat-mead and lift up your ears and get ready for my tale...

Chapter one

The Whale-road

'Aaaagghhhwwwww!' came the cry, as Lucki slipped back into the hole. He landed with his front legs on me and his back legs on Grunther, the other luckless cur chained in this watery pit.

'Thanks friend,' said Lucki, wiping the blood off his nose. 'These Irish are strong biters,' he said admiringly. As he fiddled with his snout, I heard a loud crack.

'Was that thunder?' I asked.

'Just my nose,' said Lucki. 'I think I've put the bone back in place. Can you see, Beowuff? Is it straight?'

For a battle-hardened dog of war, he spent a great deal of the time worrying about grooming. I wouldn't be surprised if he did a bit of tooth-filing as well.

I looked at his bitten nose, the bottom of it had moved to the left but the top had gone to the right.

'Grunther,' I called, 'How does Lucki's nose look?'

Grunther peered through the gloom, but that one couldn't spot a giant in a haystack. For a geld-thief and a treasure-hound, that's something of a disadvantage.

'Looks straight enough to me,' said Grunther. How straight does he want it?'

So we settled back down into the four inches of sea-water and filth that had collected in this hole where we'd been chained for days.

No matter what we did to keep warm we shivered. No matter what we did to keep dry, the scum-water leaked in. No matter how hard we tried to sleep, we were woken by the wind or by the sound of the Vikings on deck or by Bolt.

Bolt was very special. Bolt was our gaoler and he loved his job. Ever since I was captured and thrown into this bilge-hole with those two wretches I lived in fear of Bolt. I will never forget the old rat-lasher.

He was nearly as broad as he was tall and his belly never swayed more than an inch from the deck. The crew lived in terror of him, maybe because he spoke so far back in his throat that no-one could understand a single word he said. But if you did not do as he said, old Bolt would bite your ears off.

Suddenly Bolt's pug nose appeared over the edge of the hole.

'Ye Behoyewuffer,' he barked from the back of his throat.

'Me?' I asked, not wanting it to be me.

'Yeassh,' he murmured.

Every word he said seemed to begin with 'ye...'.

I stood up and shook the scum off my coat. With difficulty, I bounded up the slippery wooden slats and stuck my nose over the side

The sudden whoosh of cold air made my eyes water and my belly began to rumble.

Bolt grabbed the chain round my neck and yanked it hard, pulling the rest of me up onto deck.

He led me towards a huddle of crew and the biggest of them turned towards me.

'YeCaptain!' said Bolt, 'YeaBeoyawuffer'.

Well, I was amazed! I had finally understood a word he had said: 'YeCaptain' meant 'Captain'.

The wolfhound eyed me intently.

'C'mon over here Swede!' he said. As the Captain spoke, I stared into his gaping mouth. His breath smelled worse than a bone-digger's loot-sack. In horror, I saw that all his teeth had been replaced by bits of rusting sword blade.

The crew shuffled about nervously. A wall of black cloud was approaching and a chill wind was blowing.

Captain Wolfe grabbed my leash and pulled me up to his face, 'They say you'd better sacrifice a Swede when the weather takes a bad turn. I reckon you'll do!' he said.

Now bench-mates, as I must tell no word of a lie today, I must admit that I am about as Swedish as Bolverk the Dane. The thing is, I'd lied to the Captain about my homeland in order to put him off the scent of some other business between us. Changing my story now wouldn't save my sorry hide.

Now as luck would have it, ever since I was a pup, I've had a bit of a clever 'yap' on me and I've used it to talk myself out of many a tight spot in the past. So I knew exactly what I had to say to save myself.

Just as I opened my mouth, a spear of lightening flashed above us and we all leapt three feet backwards.

All except Captain Wolfe, who didn't even flinch. The rest of the crew stood shaking and began to howl with fear.

There was an awful moment of silence then an ear-splitting roar of thunder that got louder and louder. Then, just as we were all covering our ears, it stopped.

With an oak-splitting crash, our wave-cutter was thrown high into the air.

In the stillness that followed, the crew began to howl again. One bleating voice cried out louder than the rest.

'Wenne, wenne, wenchichenne...' it shrieked, as the lightning lit up the wide sea.

The Captain looked me in the eyes.

'Sorry it's got to be like this Swede,' he said.

'But my boat is taking water and we need to give the crew some new hope before they blame me for bringing them this far north. We must give the storm gods a treat.'

'Exactly, Captain!' I said calmly, although my heart was banging like a blacksmith's hammer. 'Thank Bodin that we have a leader like you to see us safely down the whale-road.'

'I'm glad you agree Swede!' he said, slightly surprised at my reaction. 'It'll be a treat for the great Bonefather, Lord of all the Skies and all the Seas, to make Him calm again.'

He cracked a rusty smile at me but I dearly wished he hadn't. All I could think about was how dangerous it would be to be standing near the Captain's metal teeth with the lightning-lord flinging his thunderbolts all over the place.

By now the Irish Vikings were all chanting, some of them were on their bellies, some still clinging to the oars whilst they tried to steer the ship nose-first into each mighty wave. Their song began:

'Wenne, wenne,
wenchichenne...
Bodin save us,
ravens leave us,
Abcan bronze boat,
Mac Lir lead us,
If we give you one of us...'

'Step this way then Beowuff,' said the Captain, grabbing my collar.

As I looked him in the eye, a clear thought surfaced in my wave-rattled mind. This thought flew through the muddle as straight as a spear. If one of our number was to drown himself to please the storm-gods, then it would NOT be Beowuff.

'Wait Captain! Wait!' I cried. 'Why offer the Bonefather a thieving wretch like me, when we have a true hero in our midst?'

I'd place "heroes" three rungs below Berserkers on the siege-ladder of the brainless. Typically, they're a pack of slack-witted glory hounds who dice with their lives for sport. But I knew the Captain held heroes in high esteem. So I began to lie and blather as if my very life depended on it, because it did.

'A hero?' cried Wolfe. 'Who?'

'Lucki,' I replied instantly as the next wave hit and threw us both off balance.

'Lucki has done a wide range of heroic deeds and most importantly, he's got the perfect name. Lucki by name, lucky by nature. If we get rid of him we will have much better fortune. Let's face it, ever since you captured him it's all gone a bit downhill, hasn't it?

'Are you sure that broke-nosed oaf will please the Bonefather?' snarled the Captain.

Another wave sent up a cloud of spray that drenched him from tail-tip to muzzle.

'Absolutely,' I said, 'he's fearless, I expect he'd enjoy being thrown overboard. Death wouldn't bother a dog like Luki. But perhaps it would be best not to mention my name if he asks who suggested it. It'd be more heroic if he volunteered for it himself.'

By now the sea was boiling over. The waves were capped with white and our ship was taking in water fast. I was not sure how long we could last.

On his way to find the hero, Captain Wolfe stopped.

'Are you sure that one will be enough?' he asked.

Now bench-mates, as I must tell no word of a lie today, I must confess that to my mind, there is never any sense in a slaughter like this. However, just in case there was any truth in it, we really did need to get Lucki and Grunther overboard for Gnor and Bodin and whoever else, as soon as possible!

Bolt led Lucki over to the Captain. Lucki was so big that it took four members of the crew to hold his chain. Behind him appeared Grunther, guarded by a deckpaw. Lucki looked every inch a war-dog, freshly broken nose and all, but Grunther had a sad expression, as if he had a notion about what he was about to face.

The Captain commanded the crew to stop chanting and the whole sea fell to a deathly-hush.

'Sea-dogs of Ireland, war-whelps of the whale-road, fearless battle-hounds of slaughter,' began Captain Wolfe. For a looter who specialised in sacking coastal towns, he had a fine way with words. 'I know your hearts,' said the Captain, 'I know your strength and your courage. I have seen you turn the tide red with the blood of our enemies, but now we are in the midst of a terrible storm, the like of which we have never seen before. The gods demand that we honour them...'

By the way he was talking, they could tell that he didn't mean we should honour them with sea biscuits.

The storm lessened slightly and the thunder and lightning stopped, as if the gods were listening.

'Thor is calling, and Njorthur and Mac Lir,' he said, picking up his voice again and turning to Lucki. 'Come forward you bravest of heroes and walk the road to the glory of feasting in the unseen halls...'

A huge cry went up from the crew. I joined in. The

mood lifted with the cheering and for a moment every dog felt that he would be saved.

It was only after the shouts had died down that it was clear that no-one had come forward. The crew started to glance around at us, the prisoners in chains. Lucki and Grunther. And me. For one awful moment it went even quieter. I knew I had to save myself.

'Lucki…Lucki…Lucki…Lucki…' I started to chant, desperately hoping that the war-dogs would join in. At first there was just me chanting and I realised why. They didn't know Lucki's name, so I chanted a bit louder and pointed at him. He beamed. I was lucky to have found a fool willing to give his life for his mates. Well, give his life for his captors who were probably only going to sell him into slavery.

'Lucki…Lucki…Lucki…' slowly the chant picked up and soon every dog was howling out a cheer as Lucki got ready to be thrown overboard.

'May all the gods protect you,' said Captain Wolfe. Well done! We could have been bench-mates, even though I captured you.'

Everyone wanted to sniff the hero and some tried to lick his face, but they couldn't reach.

'Good luck, great heart.' I shouted loudly, 'We'll see you in the feast hall of Valhalla.' This raised another cheer from the crew.

Lucki himself had no clue that he was expected to throw himself over the side into the seething water.

'He needs help,' I shouted. 'Help him! Help him!'

With a-one-and-a-two-and-a-three the crew cast him overboard.

'Well, Captain Wolfe-'

I was about to suggest that the Captain should say a few fitting words about Lucki as a sort of final farewell. I also wanted to line up Grunther as the next hero in case the storm didn't clear up. Then I heard a strange clanking and felt a movement like a deck-rat running along my paw.

To my horror I looked down and saw that the chain which had been coiled in a pile was disappearing over the side of the ship, still tied to that lump-wit Lucki.

The pile of coiled chain was getting smaller and soon it would have to stop. I saw a smirk the size of an elk's thigh bone come over Bolt's face. He was pointing down at my leg, for he had chained all of us three prisoners together.

I tried to run but there was nowhere to go.

The crew were all around me, pushing and jostling me. They began an awful chant,

'Beowuff…Beowuff…Beowuff…' but this time everyone joined in from the very beginning.

'Run Grunther!' I yapped, who was standing next to me.

Grunther stood gaping at me like a carp.

'Run you bilge-brain! We must wrap ourselves around the mast before we are dragged to our deaths behind Lucki.'

I pushed him, trying to stir him into action but he fell

into a pack of chanting sea-dogs, so I made off as fast as I could in the opposite direction.

The storm still raged and the boat was rocked by the violence of the waves. Just as the last yard of chain disappeared into the deep, I managed to run around the Captain at least twice.

Just what happened next, I cannot say but I ended up in a tight embrace with Captain Wolfe. At least he was so close to me that he couldn't strike me. Then, Grunther was dragged howling over the side, taking two of the crew with him.

All the while, I could hear the Captain bellowing:

'Don't just sit there, you curs! Save me! Save me!'

But whatever they did, they couldn't cut us apart whilst the ship was being rocked about.

'Looks like we are going to the Bonefather together, Captain,' I shouted through the wind.

I could taste his metal breath but I couldn't catch his words as we slipped closer and closer to the side of the ship.

If the crew wanted to save their Captain they would have to rescue me too. Alas, it wasn't that simple.

'Let Wolfe try his luck on the whale-road,' barked a voice.

'Aye, he's led us into this disaster,' said another.

'And not for the first time,' said an old sea-dog, 'he deserves to drown, the cheating fish-licker!'

'Haul hounds!' barked Bryan at the helm, 'we can't save the Captain without saving that sea-snot Beowuff first.'

Bryan seized the chain with his teeth and bit hard, trying desperately to stop his Captain from sinking below the freezing waves. But in his panic, he could hardly keep himself on board, never mind save me and the Captain. We were all being dragged down by the huge weight of Lucki, who had sunk like an anchor.

Soon Wolfe drew a breath and half-growled, half-spat these final words at me.

'A curse on you, Beowuff! And on all your cat-licking kin.'

To accuse another dog's close family of 'cat-licking' is one of the most dreadful insults under the sun. But I didn't answer, I was too busy watching the frantic faces of the crew as they peered over the side at me.

We slid silently into the deep.

Some of the crew on board had given up trying to save their Captain but others refused to let go of Wolfe's leash until there was nothing left to hang onto.

It is not the same in life bench-mates? Some of us are leapers and some of us are clingers. But either way, it matters very little, both must chase to our ends.

I can still see their longship, as it was smashed by a wave that charged up from the depths like a raging bull.

It may be that all the crew were lost as the boat turned over. Perhaps a few of them survived? Who knows? But bench-mates, most importantly, I, your friend Beowuff, am still alive and I can tell my tale to the hall.

CHAPTER TWO

BEACHED IN GUTLAND

What is the first thing a washed-up cur spat out by the sea-god feels? A sharp dig in the ribs, that's what. And then another as I felt a boot trying to lever my snout from the sand to get a better look at me.

I tried to speak but all that came out was a squirt of seawater like the death-spout of a beached whale. But there was more to come.

'Eougghhh! Beoorrghhgh!'

I raised my nose out of the wet sand only to spew once more upon the boot that had just kicked me.

'You disgusting streak of sea-snot,' boomed the voice, 'what do you mean turning up on our beach...'

'Washing up on our beach, you mean,' corrected the higher voice.

'Soiling our fair Gutland sand!' growled the second.

'Er, Pawstein?'

'What now?' barked the deep voice. 'Don't interrupt a war-dog when he's getting ready for a kill.'

'Can he actually "soil" our sand? I mean, it's sand, not soil.'

The deep voice made no answer, but I felt another hard kick crack into my ribs. Another wave of sickness came over me and I started to spout once again.

'Did you want me to kill him, or is it your turn?' asked the high voice. I felt a tail beating the sand.

I dragged my nose up to get a look at him. He was a lean, puppy-eyed mutt, and his teeth still reeked of last week's dinner. I choked in disgust.

It was all coming back to me, as I shivered on this wind-blown bay. I'd been captured by Irish Vikings, caught up in the world's wildest storm, tied to a iron-toothed loon and dragged overboard by a bad-brained Berserker. Now I'd washed up on the shores of hell.

'It's your turn to do him!' growled Pawstein. 'Get a move on.'

'Broadsword or short sword?' asked his pal cheerily.

'In the name of the Bonefather! Won't you get on with it?' growled Pawstein.

I could not protest, for I was choking on a piece of seaweed that had got stuck on its way up my gullet.

'Make haste Arnuf! If you don't do it soon, he'll be dead before you kill him! We've got ten miles of coast to patrol and the King wants a hero by nightfall.'

The soldier drew his sword from his scabbard. It looked a well-used piece with many a-notch. As he waved it at my throat, it crossed my mind that the red bits were probably blood stains rather than rust.

Oh, no, I thought, this really is the end. I am to die here on this lonely sand-heap in the swirling cold with no-one to witness my slaughter. There wasn't even time for a final howl as the soldier raised his weapon high.

'Hero?' I croaked.

'Hero,' he repeated as he brought his sword down at the very last second into the sand besides me.

'Yes! Hero!' I said desperately, eyeing the sword. 'What are you waiting for, Arnuf? Butcher this sand-rat now and have done with it.'

'You did say hero, didn't you?' I smiled, pulling the last of the seaweed from my throat.

'Yes,' said Arnuf, 'are you here because of the King's invitation? Pawstein, this is the hero we've been waiting for!'

'Hang on a minute,' said Pawstein, 'this isn't the way that heroes should arrive in our land.'

'Don't believe what the poets say, brave sea-scout,' I said, 'now, put away your weapons and no-one shall be harmed. Kill me and your king may kill you. For I am his hero. Now show me the hospitality that this land is famous for. I have had my fill of brine, so if you have any meat for your hero I will be happy to devour it.'

The big one sniffed but didn't look me in the eye.

'Smells too weak, for a hero,' growled Pawstein, suspiciously. This wire-haired brute had a good nose on him and was soon reaching for his sword again. 'I say we kill him. If you won't do it I will.'

You could hardly blame them for wanting to chop my head off for the fun of it. This beach was a sand-blasted heap, dour under the grey sky. I later discovered that the seaside is thought to be the best part of this land. There is more entertainment in the frozen hell that is Niflheim than there is in dreary Gutland.

'But hold on, Pawstein. Remember the time when you skewered that snappy fellow who had no tail? He turned out to be the Danish Ambassador,' said Arnuf.

'What else could I do?' sniffed Pawstein. 'You hit his wife with a hammer first.'

'That was an accident,' whined Arnuf.

Pawstein turned his nose to me and snapped:

'If you are a real hero, where's your blood-axe?'

He looked mightily pleased with this question.

I laughed out loud and said:

'Good shore-guard, let me tell you something. Real heroes have no need of weapons. Paws, jaws and claws are all it takes.'

Arnuf looked very impressed and yapped:

'Paws, jaws and claws! Paws, jaws and claws! Pawstein, hear that? Paws, jaws and claws!'

But Pawstein was not as meat-brained as he looked and he began to sniff at me suspiciously.

He pinned my tail with his spear-tip and I felt the sharp metal of the point delve deep into my fur.

I held his gaze with my very best 'hero's look', a look that I have spent long nights practising in the outcast's kennel. There, I learned how to look as if I treat the choice between 'life' and 'death' like the choice between 'hare' or 'rabbit' for supper.

Pawstein meanwhile prowled round me, circling and keeping the point of his spear still pinning me down as he worked out what to do next.

'See this?' I said, as I jangled the chain around my collar, in a matter-of-fact way. 'This collar was placed around my neck by a sea-serpent when she sucked me down to her watery lair. We fought for ten hours in the depths but still she could not conquer me...'

'A sea-snake?' gasped Arnuf, interrupting my stream of drivel in full flow.

'Yes Arnuf,' I said coolly, 'but no ordinary sea-snake, the Great Sea-Serpent, Sjo-Ormr, the one the sagas talk of. I have seen her, I have fought with her, I have vanquished her!'

Arnuf let out an excited yelp.

'Once you've strangled one whale-fanged sea-serpent, you've strangled them all,' I said.

'How exactly did you escape?' asked Pawstein.

'If you are going to tell a lie, tell a mighty one,' so said the unworthy Skald, Goosetongue, the 'poet' of our village. It probably wasn't his saying – nothing a Skald says is original.

What the dogs in the meat-hall crave is a plain-talking battle-hound who reels off the details of his scraps like items on a looting list. The trick is to make yourself come over like a hero, without boasting too much. No-one does it better than old Beowuff, I can spin golden falsehoods out of blades of grass. So I began...

'I was cast into the waves of the mightiest storm that the world has ever seen and I saw the shadowy figures of the axe-wielding clams rising out of the depth.'

'Clams with axes? Underwater? Grrrrrrrr!!' growled Arnuf, lapping up my nonsense like bone-jelly.

'Aye,' I continued, 'smashing through their armoured shells to their soft flesh was the hard bit. But it is simple once you get your blade in and give a real good twist.'

I borrowed Arnuf's spear to demonstrate exactly what the twist of my mighty paw could do to an armoured clam, but Pawstein stopped me.

He eyed me, scraping the sand with his spear.

'Get the blade in...?' he growled as he seized me by the chain and pulled me to meet him eye-to-eye.

'Aye,' I said.

'And twist?' he roared.

My feet were now a long way off the ground and I was struggling to breathe.

'Liar!' he spat. 'You just said real heroes don't need swords.'

He dangled me for a while and I rattled slightly.

'Who said anything about a sword?' I stammered.

'You did! You lying crab-licker,' he snarled.

'Erm, did I really?' I asked.

Arnuf raised his nose to the sky, lost in thought.

'What you said was, 'it was easy if you can get your blade in under their helmets and give a good twist.' Arnuf looked very pleased to have told the truth.

'But...,' I gasped desperately, 'that blade wasn't my sword, that was my meat-knife.'

'Save it!' growled Pawstein. 'I can't listen to any more of your drivel. Tell it to King Ruffgar.'

And with that he took my collar in his fangs, shook me roughly and threw me several feet into the air.

As I landed face-down with a thud, I was never more grateful to see the sand of friendly Gutland.

CHAPTER THREE

THE HALL OF HEORUT

The track wound onwards through the land. There is little of interest to say about the Kingdom of Gutland. In truth, describing it in an interesting way would vex even the most imaginative of Skalds. So if any of you bench-mates need to trot off to pass water, now would be an excellent time to visit the leaking post. What? So many of you? Have you been swilling meat-mead by the barrel?

While they are gone, I will tell of my journey through sunny Gutland. Here are the highlights: barren cliffs; unremarkable hills; flinty paths; stunted trees; slightly larger hills, still nothing to speak of; rocks; dark lakes; and grim mounds with a sparse covering of grass.

Ah! I see that you are all back from the leaking-post. Have you shaken your legs? Are you sure? For my cruel Lord says that it is death to dribble on his feast-hall floor. It was put in very recently I understand. Are you lying comfortably? Good – then on with the tale!

As I have already said, in order to trot through distant lands without paying for a sausage, you need to lord it like a pack-king from the sagas of old.

Here is a truth that I will never understand. If a king from a faraway land was to arrive unannounced at a royal hall, the local Lord would break out the best of his bone hoard and fill the stranger's bowl to overflowing. Yet if a boneless beggar arrived before the same king, with his clothes all in rags, and his starving belly scraping the floor, what would our warlord do then? Would he give him food and water? Would he lend him a warm woollen coat? I think not! Our Lord would throw the beggar into a fen to rot, or sell him as a slave, or let his thanes use him as a leaking post.

The point of this tale bench-mates, is that it is always important to act the casual hero. Even though I was half drowned from my sinking, and that brute Pawstein had nearly shaken the life out of me, I was not going to show any fear.

'Where are we going?' I asked heroically.

'To the hall of Heorut,' yapped Arnuf excitedly. 'Have you heard the songs tell of it?'

'Of course,' I replied. In my land they sing of nothing else.'

No word of this was true of course. I had never heard of Heorut, but when meeting a new warlord it is always wise to get a little drivelling in early. I have found that these battle-curs go all wobbly at the thought that their fame in war has spread across the seas. Even stone-faced skull-smashers never grow tired of hearing about how good they are in battle. Call me a lap-dog (go on!) but a bit of well-crafted cat-lickery means that the King will throw the bringer of good news a tasty bone or two.

'Where do you come from?' asked Pawstein in a voice which would have worried sheep in faraway fields.

I had already learned that I needed to watch my tongue with that wire-haired wretch. I knew better than to tell him of my real home, so I decided to speak falsely.

Usually lies leap off my tongue like a salmon up a stream, but for some strange reason (perhaps because of the beating he'd just given me) no ideas popped into my head this time.

Pawstein was about to repeat his question, in a lower and more menacing growl most likely, so I blurted out the first name I could think of.

'Mangefeld' I said. 'I come from dear old Mangefeld, have you heard of it?' desperately hoping he hadn't. 'It is a land of heroes.'

'For truth?' yapped Arnuf, with wide-eyes.

I have always wondered why the honest work-a-day dog, when unsure if another fellow is lying, will ask him: 'For truth?' or 'Really?' or 'Do you swear it?'

These words are about as much use as a straw shield in a dragon's nest! What weak-brained whelp would confess to their falsehood just because the other asked him if he was really lying? So when I heard Arnuf ask 'For truth?', I set out to build a mighty tower of lies, by piling on one false stone at a time.

'Aye,' I answered. 'Even the cats in my homeland go about wearing armour, in gangs.'

'They must be hard to slaughter,' said Arnuf.

'Not if you've got a hammer the size of a house.'

'He's talking fish-guts again! No one can wield a hammer the size of a house,' muttered Pawstein.

Not all stupid things come in big packages. This one was going to be trouble, but as usual, I was ready with my shining shield of nonsense.

'We don't swing the hammers ourselves,' I said. 'We've trained our giantesses to do that.'

Pawstein bristled in disbelief but his mate, Arnuf still gobbled up my rubbish like the finest deer-meat.

'It must be a joy to have giantessess at your command,' said Arnuf. 'After a raid, you could get them to pile the slaughtered up in mounds for you. I really hate that job. King Ruffgar always makes me do it.'

'That's because you're war-shy,' snapped Pawstein. 'You flee when we go on raids.'

'No I don't,' said Arnuf.

'Yes you do! You're useless at fighting. Piling up mounds of enemy dead is all you're fit for!' laughed Pawstein.

'No it's not!' yapped Arnuf in an injured tone.

'Bolt-battle,' barked Pawstein, making the smaller dog jump out of his skin. 'Arnuf the Leaky-Leg, that's what the lads in the hall call him.'

I laughed politely. There was an awkward silence. I almost felt sorry for Arnuf. With bench-mates like that, who could blame him for being war-shy? To my mind, it is no bad thing to be frightened of fighting. Some of us like to spend our evenings lazing by the fire, rather than putting towns to the torch.

Where was I? Oh yes, I was spouting some rot about giantesses.

'Aye,' I said, 'Real giantesses! Tall ones. And what's more, we feed the great she-beasts thirty squashed bulls a day, as a tribute...'

Then Pawstein stopped me with a bark.

'Behold! The mighty meat-hall of Heorut,' he cried.

'Where?' I asked.

'There of course,' growled Pawstein.

He waved his great paw in the direction of a large wooden shed that stood at the top of a moss-covered mound. The door had been painted red at some stage and you couldn't miss a huge pair of antlers at the gate. That set my belly rumbling again, for I hadn't tasted deer-stake for many a moon.

'Great, isn't it?' said Arnuf, meaning the hall.

As I can tell no lie, I'll tell you that 'Heo-Rot' would have been a better name for it.

'Where I come from, we'd keep chickens in a shed like that,' I said.

Then something unusual happened. At the word 'chickens', Arnuf dropped his spear and began to shake wildly. Pawstein's hackles stood up like wires and he bared his yellow teeth at me and twisted his features into a scowl.

'What did you say?' he growled.

I realised that I must have offended them. I was truly sorry, mainly because I wanted to taste the deer meat that the hall was famous for. While I was apologising, I saw the terror in their eyes.

'Speak not the cursed name of the egg-layers in this place!' growled Pawstein.

'What name?' I asked in wonder.

Pawstein glowered at me. I thought he was about to go for my throat.

'Come friends! Remember that I'm the guest of your King...' I said heartily.

On hearing this, the pair seemed to relax a little.

'If my words have offended you, I am truly sorry.'

'Alright,' said Arnuf

'There is no need to spit feathers at an honoured visitor,' I added.

On hearing this, Arnuf began to shake and a yellow trickle ran down the side of the mound. This was the slack-bladder that his bench-mate had spoken of.

'No more talk of egg-layers I say,' warned Pawstein. 'It is death to speak of those flapping fiends.'

'Unless the King mentions them,' added Arnuf. 'You can talk about them if he brings them up.'

Pawstein howled towards the heavens. He gave me a look as if to say that working with a wet-legged know-it-all was no job for a glory-hound.

'I shall say nothing more about them,' I promised, sighing with relief. I hadn't realised quite how close to the maw of death my fowl words had brought me.

Did you like that clever kenning bench-mates? 'Fowl words' I said, (meaning chickens) when I also meant 'foul words'. Keep up bench-mates!

27

As we drew nearer, I noticed that two young pups with brooms and buckets were busy wiping something unspeakable off the walls.

When they spotted us, something most out of the ordinary happened. One of them pointed at Arnuf, shouted something and then emptied the contents of his bucket down his own leg. His little friend fell about laughing and did the same thing.

I was about to ask about the meaning of this strange Gutland custom when two ravens, beady-eyed and black as death landed on the roof and began to stare at me hungrily.

Arnuf and Pawstein stared back at them with faces like the plague.

One of the winged-whoppers swooped low and snatched a scrap of something nameless from the gate-post. The thing in its claw was red, most likely a piece of bone-scrag, for the raven, as everyone knows, is a bird that feasts on dead meat.

'Hey Arnuf!' called one of the pups. 'Arnuf the Leak-Legged! Cover your ears quickly!'

'Why?' shouted my weak-witted guide, pulling his tunic up over his nose in a panic.

'So he doesn't see your brain!' yapped his mate. 'Ravens eat dead things, don't you know!' The two whelps rolled about on the floor laughing.

'Don't lurk there like a dirt-licker! Stone them!' barked Pawstein.

Arnuf looked at the pair of pups and sighed:

'That's a bit harsh, they were only jesting.'

'Not the pups, you limp-wit! I mean stone the ravens!' barked Pawstein in a rage.

'There's no stones,' asked Arnuf. 'Will these bricks do instead?'

Pawstein seized a clay brick in his enormous paw and was about to break it over Arnuf's nose when all of a sudden, a shadow fell across the sun. There was a terrible whooshing noise and the biggest bird that I have ever seen crashed down from the sky. The thing was practically a mountain with feathers and a beak.

The fiend stooped in a dive and snatched up one of the ravens in its scaly claws.

It is not often that I feel sorry for a bird, but I cannot forget the look on the face of that poor raven as it stared into the eyes of doom. The hunter had become the hunted. The feathered-fiend let out a booming squawk, and the smaller bird cawed back at it – as if to say "Mummy! mummy!" Then the hawk-monster cracked its beak, bit the head off the smaller bird and flapped away with its writhing body between his claws.

'Looks like you'll need bigger stones for that one,' I gasped.

'That one's friendly,' said Arnuf. 'That's Longflapper, the King's hawk. He can keep flapping for a long time,' 'That is why they call him Longflapper.'

I could think of no sensible reply to this last observation. You would have to scour all of Gutland to find a bigger fool than Arnuf.

Just then, a grizzled old fellow bounded over. He'd

seen many summers but he was still as tall as an oak, with a noble look about him.

I got ready to pour honey-tongued drivel over the Lord of this dirt-mound.

'Well-met mighty King,' I said politely. 'Aren't you going to introduce me to your Lord, fellows?'

Arnuf laughed. 'He's no King! That's old Greytongue, our Skald. He's from Icelandland, you know. '

'I'm from Iceland Arnuf,' corrected Greytongue wearily. 'Get it right for once. Who do we have here?'

'A hero,' yapped Arnuf. This one has giantesses at his command. He's come to free King Ruffgar from the curse.'

'I am called Beowuff,' I said, offering him my paw. 'At your service.'

The old rhymer jumped up and began to lick me about the face but the reek that came from his yellowed teeth would have made a war-horse dizzy.

'Greetings hero brave and tall and welcome to King Ruffgar's hall,' said the Skald.

Arnuf was impressed and howled long and loud.

'See? I told you he was good? He's from Icelandland, you know,' he said.

'Iceland,' barked the Skald. 'Remember the song I taught you: "There's only one "land" in Iceland."'

Arnuf thought about this for a moment.

'I'm sure you said it was Icelandland.'

'Please take my word for it Arnuf,' he muttered. 'I don't call you a half-half-wit, do I?'

I shot a knowing look to the old poet. Arnuf really was slack-brained – he made Gutland's limpits look educated.

'Come! Follow me,' said the Skald and he bounded up the steps and into the hall.

As I trotted inside, I noticed the wonderful smell of roasting meat. One sniff of it was enough to set my belly turning somersaults. I had eaten nothing since the Irish longship, and the filth that passed for rations on that boat was enough to make a monk turn scum-licker.

As we four walked into the hall, there came a squawk that sent me diving under a wooden bench for cover.

'What's up with you hero?' growled Pawstein.

I was embarrassed to find that the noise had come from Longflapper – the King's hawk, who had swooped into the hall through the smoke-hole in the roof and was perched on a pole.

Arnuf let out an excited bark and raced towards it.

Longflapper fixed the weak-wit with an evil glare and began to flex its claws.

'Who's a long flapper?' said Arnuf softly.

'Come away Arnuf!' cried the Skald. 'Before he bites. That hawk is a trained hunter, not a house-pet.'

'Don't worry!' he said. 'He's friendly when you get to know him.'

'Friendly?' I said in disbelief.

'Yes. He'd never hunt his uncle Arnuf! Would you boy? No you wouldn't!' cooed Arnuf in a high voice. A blast of roast meat wafted into my nostrils.

'I'm famished,' I said. 'Any chance of a bite?'

Before waiting for his answer I tore a great hunk off the deer that was roasting on a spit.

'Drop it!' growled Pawstein.

'Sorry,' said the Skald 'but the law of the hall says that no meat can be eaten till all the songs are sung.'

'No meat till song-set!' I moaned, 'No wonder old Headbiter over there looks ravenous.'

'His name is Longflapper,' said Arnuf, whining softly to the bird. At first, Arnuf's high-pitched song soothed the hawk – but suddenly, it went stock-still and cold-eyed once again, as if preparing to strike.

'Arnuf! Come away now!' cried the Skald.

But Arnuf just sat there wagging his tail.

'Beware Arnuf! He's hunting you!' he warned.

'He'd never hunt his uncle Arnie, no he wouldn't…' began Arnuf. But before the words were out of his maw, the winged terror was lurching forward to strike.

Arnuf scrambled backwards just in time. The sky-monster's bloody talons tore into the boards in the exact spot where he'd just been sitting. Luckily, Longflapper was on a leash, and flap as he might, he could not get within flesh-tearing distance of my weak-witted friend.

Arnuf didn't realise he'd had a brush with death.

'Who's a naughty hawk?' he laughed.

CHAPTER FOUR

MUZZLEGUZZLER

Although it was agreed that I was to be taken to King Ruffgar at once, I was kept waiting for what seemed like seven ages. All the while, my starved stomach was twisting like a sea-cutter in a hurricane.

Evidently, King Ruffgar kept a strict hall and the guests were led in and seated according to rank. There was a whole pack of them. Ruffgar's thanes were a rough looking crew, and they occupied the front benches. Then some of his carls were led in, to serve the thanes in various ways – doing some chewing to soften up the harder bones for the old war-dogs and so on. I have never really seen the appeal of having another dog gnaw bones on my behalf, but I perhaps I'm just not 'thane material'.

Last of all, the royals entered and sat down at a big bench in the centre, nearest the fire.

The hall fell silent as I approached King Ruffgar's bench, weak-legged and fainting with hunger.

I soon saw why they had nicknamed him 'Ruffgar The Bonegrinder'; for despite his years, his teeth looked strong enough to crush a thighbone into powder.

At his side sat the Queen, a high born dog of royal breeding, with a turned up nose and legs so slender that they looked as if they belonged on a deer.

I noticed a small creature at her side on a silver lead – it was a red squirrel. She kept feeding it treats and it danced and jigged around. I gazed at it jealously. Those treats looked tasty, and the squirrel itself would have been edible if it was roasted for long enough.

'Greetings Great Ruffgar,' I said, smiling heroically. 'Thanks for your kind invitation to the hall of Heorut. It is indeed a most mighty meat-hall.'

'I thought you said it was small,' said a puzzled voice from behind. To my dismay I found that Arnuf had trotted to my side.

'I said no such thing Lord,' I laughed nervously.

Puzzled, the King twisted his head and those eyes that had seen a thousand enemies piled up in mounds, (possibly by Arnuf) flashed at me out of grey sockets.

'Yes you did,' said Arnuf. 'You said that Heorut is the same size as the sheds in your land.'

For a simpleton, Arnuf's memory was a marvel.

My knees turned to marrow jelly and I began to quiver. I've heard of strangers being put to the sword for saying less insulting things to a king. I have never met a warlord who isn't hall-proud.

I cringed, and I thought that my life was over.

'You'll need to speak up hero,' barked King Ruffgar.

'His highness is a slight bit deaf having lost an ear in the wars with the Dragon Raiders,' began the Skald, who had joined us at the King's bench. 'It was torn from Ruffgar's royal head when the Half-Dragon's son flailed him with a burning whip.'

'Shut yer gob-hole, you slavering great muck-sniffer!' barked the King. 'I'm trying to talk tut' hero.'

Perhaps it was because I was weak with hunger but the general effect of this hoary old warrior was so terrifying that it was all I could do to stop myself rolling over in front of him right there.

I tried hard to wag my tail casually but it started to shake uncontrollably, knocking a bowl of meat-mead out of the Skald's paw. The bowl hit a nearby Berserker on the nose, he became enraged, and bit me on the paw. I leapt up in pain and crashed into the royal table.

The King's thanes who had been heavily at the meat-mead, leapt up and howled out the alarm, thinking that it was an attack by their enemies, the Hackerfolk.

King Ruffgar had little to thank me for, namely: an upturned bench; a baying pack of thanes and a Skald who'd been soaked from nose to tail in cold deer juice.

I wondered whether Ruffgar would crush my head there and then. Instead he laughed and reached out an enormous paw, his iron-claw tips scraping the wood.

'Don't worry. No harm done,' he said licking up the meat-mead with his black tongue. 'I did just the same thing myself when I was a lad, fighting the Huns.'

I panted with relief and managed a nod.

'You enjoy yourself tonight son,' said the King 'Just sort out this horrid hen business by the morning.'

Wearily, King Ruffgar rose and called on his Skald for entertainment – not always a wise decision in my experience. Many in the hall began to talk amongst themselves, laughing and lifting cups to one another, bashing them together and offering one toast after another to the glory of battle and eternal life in Valhalla. Anywhere would seem like Valhalla after Gutland.

To my horror, I saw that along with the meat, Ruffgar's cooks were serving up plates of cloudy-eyed fish. The thought of eating anything with scales makes me sick to the pit of my belly. Not only that, but it is punishable by banishment in all honourable lands. Yet by this hour, I was so hungry that I was losing my reason. My mouth was actually watering at the sight of sea-stewed, part-pickled fish!

Just then, I caught sight of the Queen. She was striking in her gold collar and flowing red robes.

She was serving up jugs of meat-mead to the most honoured of Ruffgar's warriors but when she came to the King himself, she filled up the biggest, most exquisitely decorated, most wonderfully crafted drinking horn that I had ever cast my greedy eyes upon. I was speechless and I dropped my bowl, spilling the dregs on the boards. Then the hall fell silent, as the Skald began to speak:

Hear, you, how Ruffgar,
Mighty son of Great Half-Dane,
Battle-eager warrior-hound
Renowned as far as the eagle flies,
Fed the ravens well and often
Overturned meat-mead benches
Brought back bones and plunder
And all the tribes brought him tribute.

And hear how Ruffgar,
Laden with gleaming gold
Made his faithful war-dogs rich
And no ruler gave away
More gold than Ruffgar
In sandy Gutland
In royal Ruffgar's
Kingdom of war-waging kin.

Then, learn well, how Ruffgar
Commanded a hall be built
A home for heroes called Heorut
The greatest kennel on earth,
A place of proud feasting
Where bones would pile
And Skalds could sing
Every night of every year for evermore.

And no-one has never worn
The weapons of war more proudly
Than Bodin's havoc-bringer,
Mighty Ruffgar, nor drunk
So deep as Gutland's greatest
Guzzler from Gutland's greatest
Treasure, the rune-bound
Magic horn made by Weyland,
The most cunning of metal-makers
in a secret forge
Made this horn at night, while the blindfolded poet

37

Sang the charms of Sigurd
And Skirnir and the blazing fires
And told all this in runes
Written in gold and blood
To make the magic Muzzleguzzler,
A horn like no other ever made.

As the old Skald came to a halt, I was carried away with the beauty of his words. No-one else took much notice. Perhaps they'd heard it all before?

I couldn't take my eyes off the Queen. In her paw she was holding Muzzleguzzler – the very horn that the old Skald was describing in his poem. It was magnificent. I started to strain to remember the Skald's verse and thought that if I could catch the meaning and remember the lines I would have the knowledge to become the owner of that horn.

I made myself a promise, Muzzleguzzler might have secret magical runes on it and it may have been made by the master smith Weyland himself – but I would make it mine!

Everything started to happen quickly. I watched intently as old Ruffgar casually picked up the horn and used it to scratch his ragged ear. He'd forgotten its worth and beauty long ago. I would take much better care of it. In my paws it would once again be magic and come to life. I am breathless and in love. No price can be put on a thing so unique, so exquisite. I don't want to think about what it might be worth in bones because no amount of plunder could buy it.

'Nice words eh? Good old Greytongue, he comes from Icelandland, you know,' says Arnuf, moving up next to me.

I did not answer for I was busy working out how to move Muzzleguzzler to a more loving home – mine!

'Did you know that he can rhyme on and on and on till sunrise,' said Arnuf. 'He often does.'

'How in the name of Gnor's flashing thunderbolts do you get him to shut up?' I asked.

'We don't bother, we just ignore him,' said Arnuf.

'If he keeps on till dawn, I'll die of hunger,' I cried.

King Ruffgar thumped a paw on the table. Those around me fell silent. You could hear a pin drop, which on a straw floor was pretty unusual.

'Another lay, my Lord?' asked the Skald. 'Perhaps the Saga of Sven the Sarcastic? Or his half-brother, Carl the Limper?'

'Sorrowful histories! How delightful!' called the Queen. 'Can we have the next instalment of the one about Limping Carl? I hope his hind legs get better in time for his marriage to Gunhild Gruntmother.'

'Suffering Swedish sagas!' moaned King Ruffgar, 'Don't tell me there's more of the beggars?'

The Skald looked wounded.

'There are one hundred and seventy-nine in this story cycle, my Lord, and your father knew them all by heart, and his father before him...'

'And his father before him,' added Arnuf.

'Save us from the dull Swedes!' howled Ruffgar.

I laughed loudly at this and toasted the King.

'Why not tell us a tale of your land hero,' sneered the Skald bitterly, 'if you think you can do any better?'

'Good idea,' shouted the King, dealing the table a hammer blow with his iron-clad paw. 'What tale are we having? Is it the one about the whelks?' asked the King, bringing the hall to silence.

'You mean the clams, mighty Lord' I said.

The thought of a hero battling whelks got Ruffgar's pack laughing but the old warlord was not amused.

'Are you trying to be funny hero?' he growled, bashing the table with his paw again. This time no-one copied him. Sick with fear, I tried not to quiver.

'Of course not, great King, but I fought huge sea-clams on my journey here, not whelks.' I said.

Everyone else in the hall looked at one another and was not sure what to do.

'Ha ha ha,' said Ruffgar after a moment, 'huge sea-clams indeed.' Then he turned to the Skald, eyeing him with intent, 'And where are your sagas of heroes who fight huge shellfish and survive?'

'Well, my Lord...' began the Skald, but he was interrupted by the King.

'Listen and learn Greytongue,' said Ruffgar. 'The young hero will entertain us.'

Every paw in the hall banged on every table and the chant of my name went up, ringing through the rafters and out into the night. King Ruffgar called for silence and all eyes fell on me.

'Poems are not really my style, your Horness...I

mean, your Highness. Besides, nothing much happens in my land,' I whined.

'Nonsense!' roared Ruffgar.

'Lots of things happen in his land,' called Arnuf in his usual enthusiastic way, 'they've got gangs of armoured cats and cat-hammering giantesses!'

I moaned aloud. That midden-brain had the memory of a whale-fish. You couldn't say a single sentence to him without him bringing back every last word of it.

The whole hall were hammering the benches but I wasn't in the mood for it. Hunger pangs were making my guts leap about like rats on a fireship.

'Sorry, Lord, but I am a very poor Skald...'

'It doesn't have to rhyme, just make sure there's no Swedes in it. If it's a choice 'tween cat-hammering and those beggin' Swedes then bring on the cats any day.'

There was no way out. If only I hadn't laughed so loudly at the King's remarks about Sven the Sarcastic. I racked my hungry brain but nothing came to mind.

'In my land,' I began, 'we say, "warriors' feat, Skald's meat."'

There were only a couple of nods of understanding around the hall of Heorut and after a lengthy pause, the King laughed and banged his horn on the table.

I winced. I'd better keep it simple then: blood, battle and bones and the like. So I began:

> *Before I do feats,*
> *Bring me some meat!*
> *Bake me a pie*
> *And I won't be war-shy*

Pass me a plate,
And I'll smite foes with hate.
Send me some steak,
Many lives I will take.
Cut me a chop
And I'll hack till I drop.
Bring out a trough full
And you'll make me wrathful!
Wheel out a cart full,
In war I'll be artful!
Before a big battle,
Roast all of your cattle!'

Well, the hall erupted. Howls of praise, tankards banging, helmets bashing tables. The Fighting Dogs of Ruffgar really loved their food. At the King's command, a sizzling mound of deer steaks was placed at my feet.

I saw one face slink into the shadows, its eyes filled with envy. It was the Skald. I'd made my first enemy at Ruffgar's court.

'Good luck tonight lad!' laughed the King, rising from the bench. 'When they wipe the blood off the walls, make sure it's not yours.'

Ruffgar slapped my back, taking his leave, but he needed the support of four retainers, one under each leg, to get him out of the hall. 'It's an old war-wound,' he explained as they carried him off, 'not the meat-mead.'

As the King left, he had a final word in my ear: 'No offence meant son. But some of these heroes they're sending me are about as much use as a linen helmet.

Anyone would think that they're afraid of pain. Spineless foe-fleers, the lot of them. Just you sort the cursed hen out for me and you can have your pick of treasure.'

Ruffgar turned to the Skald. 'Swedish sagas!' he growled as they carried him out of the hall.

A presence at my neck made me jump, I turned around and there was the Queen still carrying the mighty horn Muzzleguzzler. She smiled in a tired way.

'Good luck Beowuff,' she said, softly, 'if you are as much a hero as you seem, and you fight as well as you rhyme then we hope to see you on the morrow.'

Her teeth shone like stars in the gloom but even they couldn't match the sheen of the gold engravings and dancing figures on the horn she still carried.

The servants were extinguishing the lights one by one and for a moment I imagined reaching out and taking Muzzleguzzler from the Queen and saying a quiet 'Thank you,' and walking off into the night.

Just then, there was a commotion at the head of the corridor and King Ruffgar appeared again, without his helpers this time.

'Wife!' he barked. 'Wife! Don't forget me horn.'

The Queen seemed caught between wanting to talk to me and her duties to her Lord and King.

'I did enjoy your poem about the meat,' she yawned, and with that she trotted off towards the doors.

CHAPTER FIVE

THE HORRID HEN

Ruffgar's words echoed around my head: 'Have your pick of treasure.'

I pushed some fallen drinking bowls out of the way so that I could lie down on a bench. Did he mean that I could have whatever I desired without having to steal it? What was this 'cursed hen' that he kept talking about? How could a single chicken be the cause of such havoc when Ruffgar's retainers were some of the meanest wardogs this side of the Kennels of the Dead?

None of it made sense and no matter how hard I tried, my thoughts always came back to the King's words, 'Your pick of treasure.' That meant only one thing to me, the magical, golden horn Muzzleguzzler. Would Ruffgar gift his prized possession to a chancer like me?

I stared into my meat-mead cup, watching the reflections of the flickering lights of the hall in the surface of the sickly liquid.

I was lost in a sort of dream and the sounds of the hall grew dim, but I thought I saw a squirrel appear out of nowhere. It scampered as squirrels do in that way that means we dogs of war simply have to chase them. It ran up the wall easily, crept along a rafter, leapt over the joint and then jumped to the next rafter. Finally, it crouched above me, looking down and tilting its head to the side. Then it started to speak.

'Who are you? The latest hero for the treasure, eh?' it chattered.

'Who are you?' I growled.

As I rule, dogs of war don't usually talk to squirrels, they chase them and tear them apart, for sport.

With a soft bounce, it landed right next to me.

'Call me Rati, I'm the Queen's pet, so to speak. Here for your big night are you? I don't want to worry you, but I've seen many heroes come to this hall. I hope you're braver than Slav the Nailor. He took a real hammering. To win out, you must see the monster for what it really is.'

'Eh?' I cried, rather surprised to find myself talking to a squirrel. In my land this was one step up from death-mound sniffing.

Rati hadn't finished yet.

'Here are some more wise-words for you,' he laughed.

He who travels widely needs his wits about him.
The stupid should stay at home.

With that epigram, Rati was gone into the darkening roof-space.

I looked around the hall and found it nearly empty. No one else seemed to have noticed the talking squirrel as they went about the business of tidying up after the merry-making of the evening. Though how they could make merry when I was about to have my body parts used for wall-decoration was beyond me. I needed help before I faced havoc, gore and certain death.

In a far corner the Skald was droning on earnestly to Arnuf. Two or three servants were sweeping the floor. And some carls were dealing with the last of the sprawling figures as they made their way to their beds. Lucky mutts – at least they'd be waking up alive!

My nose had sank into my meat-mead bowl and I was beginning to think dark thoughts when the Queen suddenly appeared before me, shining and elegant, carrying a torch of burning rushes.

'Good Queen, well met,' I said.

'Call me Ethelpelt, please,' she said, almost purring. 'My real name is Wealhtheow but Ruffgar begged me to change it after we got married. He slurs his words when he's nervous you see.'

I smiled at her politely.

'Do not be so sad hero, great deeds are in front of you.'

'Queen Wealtht...,' I began, but I had to give up midway through so as not to cause offence. 'My Queen,' I started again, 'may I have your counsel for a moment?'

Was it my imagination, or did she look pleased to be giving counsel to a hero such as myself?

'My hero,' she said sniffing me delicately, 'I'm glad you are still here. My Lord Ruffgar has sent me to ask which weapon you prefer.'

She smiled at me patiently but before I could answer, the Skald came bounding past us, chasing after Arnuf. Ethelpelt hailed them, and they stopped in their tracks.

'This brave young hero was just wondering which weapon he should use against the creature that will come to Heorut tonight with evil intent. King Ruffgar wishes to furnish him with the finest arms in Gutland.'

Before I could reply, Arnuf jumped up excitedly. 'Beowuff has no need of weapons,' he yapped.

The Queen tilted her head and looked puzzled. 'Really?' she exclaimed.

'Well...' I began.

'Paws, jaws and claws are all it takes,' Arnuf interrupted. I could have split his weak-witted skull with the back of a battle-axe.

'Really?' exclaimed the Queen with unquestioning admiration. 'That's impressive. The other heroes asked for half our armoury. But look what happened to them.'

The three of them burst into laughter. They only stopped when they saw the look in my eyes.

'Are you sure you don't need anything Beowuff?' said Queen Ethelpelt in a concerned voice.

'Well, I suppose a battle-hardened shield might be handy – just to keep the blood off your highness's wall-hangings, you understand,' I said.

'Is that all? Nothing else?' asked the Queen.

Then I had a magnificent idea.

'Bring me gold,' I announced, 'as much gold as possible. For it is said that gold is a proven charm against this sort of curse.'

'Aye, certain sagas sing of this,' said the old Skald, giving me a curious look.

'Very good,' said the Queen, 'if the sagas sing of it then so shall it be. Anything else?'

'Meat,' I said, unhesitatingly.

Have you not had sufficient?' asked the Queen. We have roasted thirty stags for your feast tonight.'

'The meat is for bait, dear lady,' I explained, ignoring the Skald. 'Hunger means nothing to me, nor carnage nor death.' I paused for effect. 'So bring over the biggest pile of the tastiest cuts that can be found – and none of your scrag-ends either,' I added, eyeballing the Skald, 'for monsters do not dine on morsels.'

'You will not need meat to lure the hen-fiend,' said the Skald.

'My dear Greytongue,' I began, 'I am the hero and you are the rhymer. And I say we will need meat.'

'Very well you shall have it,' agreed Queen Ethelpelt graciously.

'But we have never needed bait to lure the feathered-one-who-cannot-be-named before,' snapped the Skald.

There was absolute silence in the great hall and the hackles rose on every one of us. The Queen's torch spluttered in the gloom and we were plunged into darkness. The Skald chose his moment and spoke in a voice both deep and grave.

'He did not need bait when he swooped like a sea-eagle and gutted the Lords of Gothland. The flesh of the King's kinsmen carried off in the night is all the bait needed to tempt that blood-beaked burglar.'

Arnuf let out a very high-pitched whimper and there was the unexpected sound of trickling water.

'Arnuf!', snapped the Queen.

'Sorry,' said Arnuf.

'Ahh, Greytongue,' I began, addressing the Skald, 'you seem to know a lot about the fiend's night attacks.'

'Aye,' he said, with great pride, 'I am composing a whole saga about it. It will be three days in the telling. It will establish my fame until the end of time...'

For one hideous moment I feared that the old bull-borer would begin it there and then.

'But that's not the worst of it,' said a voice so frightened that I hardly recognised it. It was Arnuf's.

We all waited for an explanation.

'There's the curse as well,' he howled.

'What curse?' I asked, becoming more worried.

'Swelling up like that must be horrible.'

'Aye,' agreed the Skald sadly, 'remember Ivar, the Coarse Norselander from Orkney.'

'Poor Ivar,' said the Skald, 'but we should not talk of him,' gasped the Queen.

'That's not fair,' I said, 'you can't tell half-tales, What happened to Ivar? Will the same thing happen to...me?'

'Poor Ivar swelled up like a bladder,' said the Skald, gravely. 'They were calling him Ivar the Inflated by the end. He was so bloated that he was towed back to Kirkwall behind his own longship.

'He got bloated and was floated?' I gasped in dread.

'Aye, for truth. He was moored in the harbour for three weeks before the elders of the town found a way of letting him down gently,' said the Skald.

The Queen howled as if in real pain, 'Why does this bird torment us so?'

'Why does the carrion-bird peck first at the eye?' asked the Skald in sympathy with the Queen. 'Why does the salmon leap up the stony stream?'

'Why does the seagull follow the longship?' added Arnuf.

'Your wisdom is growing, young Arnuf!' said the Skald, slightly surprised. 'Why indeed?'

'Why do the brainless ask questions that are pointless?' I muttered.

'Well, go on. Tell us the answers then,' demanded Queen Ethelpelt. 'Why?'

'The whole point is, dear lady, that it matters very little..' said the Skald, triumphantly.

'I think it matters rather a lot,' said the Queen, sweetly and persistently.

'If we knew why the seagull follows the longship, we could shoot him in the gullet,' added Arnuf, who had regained his usual enthusiasm for everything.

'Well said!' laughed Ethelpelt, 'but now I must retire to the Royal Kennel for the night.'

'Stop! Wait!' I cried nervously. 'About this curse...'

'There is no more time to speak of it, we must away from the hall of Heorut for The Cursed Hour is nearly upon us. Your Majesty – remember to have the gold brought here as soon as possible,' said the Skald.

The Queen wished me luck as she took her leave.

'Could you send that meat? As a backup?' I called.

'Come along, Arnuf,' said the Skald, 'you can't stay here – we have to leave this hero to his fate.'

From the nearest bench came a scraping and a rustling sound like there was someone trapped beneath it.

'Off you trot!' called a voice from under the bench. It was Pawstein, Arnuf's fellow shore-guard, who had clearly taken an awful lot of meat-mead. 'I've been listening to you trump-hounds all night and I never heard such war-shy talk. It makes me sick.'

From the doorway a light appeared. The Skald had returned because of the commotion.

'I'm not war-shy,' said Arnuf, 'but no-one survives when the fiend attacks.'

'Listen to you! Wiggling like a worm in the face of a little danger,' laughed Pawstein.

'I'm not battle-shy, I tell you!' repeated Arnuf. 'I may not be the biggest dog in the hall, but it's like that saga, sometimes small dogs can have the heart of a...'

'Maggot!' growled Pawstein, baring his teeth. 'You're worm-hearted! Always have been, always will be!'

Pawstein grew fiercer in that too-many-mead-cups-spoiling-for-a-fight way that I have seen so many times. Then something strange happened. Arnuf rose to his full height, stretching out on his toes, and reached up to Pawstein's thick iron-studded collar.

'No, I'm not,' he answered calmly, looking straight into Pawstein's bleary eyes.

Pawstein glared at him, and let out a cruel laugh.

'Prove your courage then,' he scoffed. 'Stay the night in this hall with the hero.'

'All right then,' said Arnuf, without the slightest tremor in his voice, 'I will.'

'That really won't be necessary,' I said, for I had absolutely no intention of staying the night in the hall. I had instead, been forming a plan that would put me safe on a longship full of the King's gold. At the heart of it were large helpings of sneaking, theft and treachery.

Only a fool would stay in the hall when the horrid hen appeared. Not I! Hendel could use someone else for flesh-ripping practice.

'Are you sure you want to stay Arnuf?' asked the Skald with concern. 'It is oft said that…'

'No!' barked Arnuf, 'You can't change my mind. I'm staying. Only death will move me from this spot.'

Oh, Arnuf! If you died tonight, the world would lose a solid gold clod-sniffer. I could have wept.

'Give my regards to the hen-fiend!' called Pawstein as he crashed out of the door. 'I hope you've got a mop handy, Arnuf here gets wet-legged when battle calls.'

The only thing that cheered me was the arrival of the soldiers with bags of gold coins, by order of the Queen. There didn't seem any shortage of the stuff so I got them to put it by the door. I didn't want to add to the distance when I made my escape.

When the soldiers had finally left I noticed that Arnuf had been true to his word and was still with me.

'Never mind what Pawstein said. We're bench-mates now. We'll look out for one another. Drink this, it will give you courage.'

I passed him my meat-mead and it seemed to revive his spirits a little.

'Thanks,' he said.

After he took a drink I urged him on. 'Come on, warrior, drink up, there's a long night ahead. A true war-dog cares nought for death or life, it is all the same to him. Drink all you can find and when we are done we will wait for the feathery-fiend side by side.

I placed another cup of meat-mead in front of Arnuf and considered what to do next. Would it be best to knock this simpleton into tomorrow with a blow from behind and make a run with the gold? Or should I go to the Queen's chamber and steal the famous horn Muzzleguzzler, leaving Arnuf to his fate with the horrid hen? I was just looking for something heavy and blunt for head-cracking purposes, when I heard another noise in the doorway.

The meat had arrived. At least eight platters of the juiciest, tenderest-looking cuts I had seen in a very long while. Was there no end to Ruffgar's hospitality? I couldn't leave Arnuf with all this pleasure so I tore into the meat-plates like a fox in a hen-house.

CHAPTER SIX

THE MAUL IN THE HALL

When I woke up, I found that the fire was dead, the meat was all gone and the wooden benches had been turned over in disarray. I racked my mead-muddled mind to remember what had happened during the night. But try as I might bench-mates, I could not remember anything.

If it was not for the amount of mead I had consumed the night before, I would have said that a witch had hexed my brain, or an enchanter had stolen my memories away.

I decided that a walk would clear my thoughts but when I rose it felt like there was a wolf-pack howling in my skull. When I stood up it felt as if a meaty longship had beached itself in my bowels. Looking down at my tunic, I saw that my belly had bloated up like a dead whale-fish. In horror, I rubbed at my gut. My food-sack was three times its normal size and practically scraping the floorboards.

Then I remembered the curse of Hendel.

The horrid hen must have put a curse in my belly! It had come in the night and flapped back to its murky mere with Arnuf in its twisted beak. Well hall-pals, as I have said, pity does not come easily to me. But as I stood alone in the wrecked hall, I thought of that poor slack-brain Arnuf. He prattled a lot, but even a cur like that didn't deserve to be cursed. I could have shed tears for him, but villains like me don't cry. Then I remembered the gold that could have been mine – and I began to weep buckets.

'Gold by the cart full! Coins by the bowlful!' I moaned. 'Treasure that could have been mine! Now it is all gone!'

I banged my head hard against the bench, in despair. I only did this once, for it was a hard bench.

War-dogs – heed my warning. If you are going to beat your head against a bench, have a care that it is not made of hard wood. If possible, go forth and head-bang against a bench made in Sweden, for the furniture of this land is so feebly put together that it often falls apart by itself.

Wincing in pain, I leapt up and began to search the hall for gold. Even a stray coin or two would have bought me passage from this waste-land! I was sick to the gut-sack of Gutland and all who lived in it.

When I was sure that there was no gold about the place, I clutched my belly and howled in despair.

'Morning,' came a voice from the corner.

I stood speechless as a figure leapt up from behind a large pile of shields and bounded towards me with a smile. It was my muddle-minded bench-mate Arnuf, not beaked to pieces by the hen-fiend, but standing here before me.

'I could murder a kipper,' he said. 'I don't suppose

you've got any?'

My poor stomach twisted into knots at the thought of fish and I cursed him for the pain he'd caused me.

'Arnuf! Stop thinking of your stomach and spare a thought for mine,' I moaned as I pulled back my cloak to reveal the swollen mound of my belly.

'Impressive!' said Arnuf. 'And all bought and paid for, as my grandfather used to say.'

'Help me! By Gnor's bolts! Is there no one in this land that can mend my aching guts?' I begged.

Arnuf stopped and scratched his ear.

'There's old Leatherbucket the butcher. He's always got a lot of guts lying about his shop,' said Arnuf. 'He keeps them in leather buckets, you know.'

'I am cursed by Hendel! Do you not see? Take me to a healer before I swell up like Ivar the Inflated.'

On hearing this, Arnuf became distracted.

'The Curse! Take Courage! Take Courage!' he cried – running about the hall like a hare on fire.

In the end, I had to get a lead on him, tie him to a bench and get him biting on a shield in order to calm himself down.

'Think Arnuf! Think! I am sick and I need a physician, a doctor, a healer, a bone-setter…

'A wizard? A horse-doctor? A midwife?' he cried.

'No!!!' I screamed as my poor guts squirmed like a sea-squid. 'I beg you to think carefully! For my very life depends on this. When you are ill, who is it that makes you well?'

CHAPTER SEVEN

THE HOUND OF HEALING

Where are all of you carls going in such a great hurry? Are you off to the leaking-post again so soon? Perhaps you need to see a healer yourselves bench-mates, if you cannot hold your meat-mead and must go dashing off every five minutes?

I'll grant that this part of my tale is only describing my journey to the worm-worn hole of the Hound of Healing, but hurry back or you'll miss the good bit that's coming up next. There's a double deadly poison on its way.

It was with small cheer that I found myself struggling after Arnuf, down a little-worn deer track which led away from his settlement. I learned that The Hound of Healing lived some miles past Ruffgar's hall, in a fly-infested dell by the mere, on the near side of a fetid fen.

Gutland is not best know for its healers, as I was about to find out. The locals are a hardy pack, and they rarely fall ill. If they take a bad wound in battle, they'll end up lying down in a death-mound rather than in a sickbed.

Weeds had grown up all along the way and sniffs at regular intervals revealed that this was a path seldom travelled, and seldom scent marked.

It was broad daylight – well, what passes for daylight

in gloomy Gutland anyway. As I toiled onwards, the road led down and down into a dark and dingy dell.

The woods thickened and the shadows drew in so that I could barely see the white tip of Arnuf's tail in front of me. He is very proud of that tail-tip, but if you ask me, any number of seagulls could have given him a marking like that.

The forest was dark; (what forests are light in these tales?); the shadows were long; (who ever heard of a short-shadow) and there were fell voices on the air (headless ravens and other wood spirits no doubt).

I staggered along behind Arnuf, clutching at my blown-up belly until I could go on no longer.

'Arnuf!' I cried. 'You are killing me! Do not run so fast. I am sick, and I can't keep up. Tell me how much longer must we go on? Must we trot on through this night-forest till the end of days?'

'Here we are,' he said.

Before us stood a wood-stump kennel, of the very strangest sort. It was covered in moss and surrounded by a ring of sun-bleached deer antlers. The door itself was made of wood, but it was riddled with tiny worm-holes.

From somewhere far inside, a hollow voice cried:

'Eeeeeeenter!'

'She's in there,' said Arnuf.

'Who's in there?' I asked.

'The Hound of Healing of course,' said Arnuf.

Well bench-mates, when I was a young pup my

father's father used to gather us all around the long fire and while away the happy hours with inappropriate tales. One of his favourites was called 'Hole-Swallower' about a traveller who stopped to rest by the entrance of a small cave, just the same size as the one at the back of our sleeping place. The traveller heard a voice coming from it that bade him to 'Enter!'

He refused at first but the voice was persuasive and promised to take him to meet the mighty Bonefather himself, and show him his famous long-kennel with the great big Bone Hoard and all. It even promised that he could visit the trading hut afterwards and pick himself out a trinket like a little Gnor's hammer brooch to take home with him.

These promises lured the unwary traveller into following the stranger down the tunnel-mouth. He disappeared down that gloomy shaft, and he never saw the light of day again. For the hole was alive! It had swallowed him, you see.

So as you can imagine, I have a terror of caves, amongst other things, and nothing, not even the Great Sea-Serpent, Sjo-Ormr herself would suck me down one. And bench-mates, she has a very powerful set of suckers.

'Eeeeeeeenter!' called the voice again. This was followed by a cackle that echoed up through the hole-mouth.

'Arnuf,' I moaned, 'Arnuf my friend. Do your old hen-battling hall-pal a favour would you?'

'What?' he asked.

'Pop down there and bring me back a potion to heal my bloated belly. Anything that the old crone thinks would...'

'The Hound of Healing, you mean,' corrected Arnuf. 'And she is not an old crone.'

'Really?'

'Really,' he said. 'In fact, she has a beautiful coat of ruby-red that shines in the sunlight, if you are ever lucky enough to see it.'

'My mistake!' I said. 'I meant, go and fetch me anything! Anything that this ruddy-coated wonder thinks will ease my pain and reduce the size of my... you know.'

Arnuf considered this.

'Alright, he said I'll do it!'

'You have my thanks,' I said. 'Now hasten, 'ere I burst my bloated gut-bag!'

With that he stuck his nose down the hole and let out a bark.

'Seeeeeeeerrrrrrrvice!' he howled.

'Eeeeeeeeeeeeeeenter!' it called back.

'We cannot eeeeenter, for we are too biiiiig for your hooooole,' said Arnuf.

From out of the tunnel-mouth beside the tree hopped a very strange creature, familiar and yet unfamiliar.

Was it bigger than a elf you ask? I cannot say, since elf-measuring has not been one of my pastimes. However, it had a very strong musky scent to it, unlike any dog that I have sniffed. And sniffing is something of a favourite hobby of mine. The tang of it was quite peculiar. I wished that it would come out into the light, so I could get a proper look at it. But the hound was wary and would not move from the mouth of its strange smelling den.

'What dooooooo you waaaant?' called the creature.

I got a look at the beautiful coat of ruby-red that Arnuf had been talking about. I fear that it looked a bit mangy.

'Oh clever Hound of Healing!' cried Arnuf. 'We are here for your wisdom.'

'And your medicine!' I growled, clutching my guts as they roared like a walrus. 'And potions.'

'Oh red-coated hound, known to be wise,' said Arnuf, 'this hero has need of your herb-lore.'

'And if possible, the herbs themselves,' I added. For I did not fancy the idea of grubbing around that dingy dell on a pointless quest for scarcely known leaves or obscure field mushrooms.

It is well known that one of the oldest tricks in the 'healer' game is to send the patient off searching for ingredients. Give 'em a long enough list and by the end of it their headache will be gone of its own accord.

As I explained my symptoms, the Hound of Healing scrabbled around, running up and down her dank tunnel. For some time she tinkered about with her bags of herbs, her fairy dust and her pots of potions in the fiddling manner that they seem to teach them at healer's school.

For myself, I find fairy dust one of the most annoying substances under the stars. The leaf pouches that it is kept in are likely to split and attract wasps and biting flies.

The Hound let out a high-pitched keening noise, the sort of sound you get if you prod a medium-sized tomcat with a thorny branch.

'Hark!' said Arnuf. 'She sings the song of healing.'

When the healer scurried back up the tunnel, she had a mouthful of something, but she spat it out at our feet.

'See!' said Arnuf in wonder. 'She spits the spit of healing!'

The Hound of Healing then licked it back up from the stony ground.

'Look!' cried Arnuf. 'She licks the lick of healing!'

'Noooo!' said the Hound. 'Thaaaaat was my lunch.'

'Your lunch?' I said, trying hard to hide my disgust.

'It neeeeeeeeds chewing twice,' she explained.

When the Hound of Healing had finished mixing up her herbs, she placed a pile of leaf wraps at the tunnel's mouth for me.

'Eaaaaaat one of these at sunrise and another at sunset.'

'My thanks!' I said. 'But what should I do? I mean, what if I go on bloating and I swell up and my gut-sack actually bursts?'

'Eaaat two,' she advised.

I nodded my thanks and turned back to the track.

'What do we owe you, oh fair Hound of Healing?' asked Arnuf as we were leaving.

That fool! I could have bitten his spit-stained snout off! There we were, our business done and almost away down the track, and Arnuf had decided to bring up the matter of payment.

Desperately trying to change the subject, I called:

'Farewell wise hound. King Ruffgar sends his regards.'

'How is old RRRRRRRRuffgar?'

'He's very well, thank you!' I shouted back. By now I'd started to trot and I was building up to a bound whilst trying not to look as if I was running away.

'Is he still cursssssssed?' wailed the Hound.

'He's very well, apart from the curse, I mean,' I answered.

'Take thissss!' called the Hound of Healing, springing out from her hole to pass me a white packet.

Panting for breath, she seemed to be able to get her words out easier. 'It is a herb called Hensbane, deadly to dogs but double-deadly to hens, even enchanted ones.'

'Double deadly!' cried Arnuf in excitement.

'Hen-killing potion you say?' I asked. 'That's very good of you.'

Just as we were about to leave, a lonely sunbeam found its way through the tangle of branches and for the first time, I understood what sort of creature The Hound of Healing really was.

CHAPTER EIGHT

A DREADFUL BEATING

As we made our way back to the hall of Heorut, Arnuf was bubbling with excitement.

'She came out of her hole for us!' he said excitedly. 'She doesn't usually do that. And she actually sung her song for us. I love the Hound of Healing.'

'The Fox of Healing,' I corrected.

'The Hound of Healing, you mean,' he replied.

'Arnuf. She's a fox,' I sighed.

'She is not a fox!' he barked in an injured tone.

'She lives in a den in the woods...'

'That's the Hole of Healing,' he corrected.

'She's got a mangy ginger coat...'

'No, a fair coat of ruby-red,' he answered.

'That big thing sticking out from her bottom,' I said. 'Know what that's called?'

'A broomstick?' asked Arnuf.

'A brush, Arnuf! All foxes have them instead of tails. You'd know that, if you weren't as wet as a whelk at high tide.'

'The Hound of Healing is a fox!' yapped Arnuf in surprise. 'Just wait till I tell the hounds in the hall about this!'

'That wouldn't be wise,' I warned. 'Bearing in mind what hounds are known to hunt for.'

I have no great love of foxes, but the potion that the

healer had given me might be the only way to deflate my swollen gut-sack.

'Come Arnuf,' I said, prodding at my churning stomach to see if it was improving. 'We must return to tell the King of my success in battling the Horrid Hen.'

'Success?' cried Arnuf in amazement. 'So you mean that we beat the hen-fiend?'

'Of course we did bench-mate,' I replied. 'Don't you remember?'

'Er, not really,' said Arnuf. 'But I don't usually remember much after a long night at the mead-bench.'

We walked back through the dank woods, with the mist rising, towards the hall of Heorut.

As we drew nearer to Ruffgar's stronghold, I decided to have a word with Arnuf about foxes and hens.

'Bench-mate,' I began softly, 'most loyal friend, much has passed between us that has been surprising and also somewhat distressing. I am very grateful for your support in times of difficulty and danger.'

I slapped him on the back in true war-dog fashion.

'Don't mention it,' he replied.

'Exactly,' I said after a pause, 'as wiser dogs than me have said, some words are better left unspoken.'

I eyed him closely.

'Yes,' said Arnuf, far too quickly.

'Do you understand me?' I asked, looking at him with a penetrating glare.

'Fire!' he barked suddenly. 'Fire! Fire!'

I span around to look for the cause of the panic but

nothing was aflame and there was no smell of smoke.

'Fire?' I yelped in confusion. 'What do you mean Arnuf?'

'That's one of those words, that should be left unspoken,' he explained.

'What?' I spluttered in bewilderment.

'King Ruffgar told me that if I ever bark "Fire!" in a crowded hall again, he'd roast me over one. Is that what you mean?'

'Arnuf,' I growled softly, 'there are times when it is wise to know about something but not to tell the whole hall about it. For example, if Ruffgar's pack ever find out that the Hound of Healing is in fact a Fox of Fakery they would doubtless savage her to death for the sport of it and then where would we be?'

'Where would we be?' he asked.

'In trouble,' I sighed. 'In fact we'd be up the city walls without a siege ladder. Unless you know of another place in Gutland where we can find medicine for my bloated belly?'

I waited to allow my words of counsel to sink in, but they flapped around his head like a pigeon in a grain-store. After a moment he tilted his head again.

'You mean...' he began.

'Arnuf,' I said firmly, 'whatever happens, keep your mouth shut about the fox, and about the curse and about my victory over Hendel – in fact, it might be better if you don't speak for the next month.'

'Uh?' said Arnuf, letting out a whimpering noise

which he made at times of great concentration, like when he was trying to remember the number that came after three.

When we reached the great hall of Heorut, the doors were flung open and we were ushered in by the gate-guards. Within moments we were brought before King Ruffgar, who had sent his scouts out to search for us. Soon the hall was packed with the war-dogs of Gutland, hanging on our every word. It was a bit of a worry, even for a liar-lord like myself.

'So hero, have you rid my hall of the Horrid Hen?' asked Ruffgar.

'Aye my Lord,' I replied. 'I have.'

Ruffgar began to bang the table with his iron-clad paws. The hall shook as every thane, dog of war and carl joined in with their king. It was utterly deafening and nothing I could do or say could bring them to a halt. After a few minutes the King called for silence.

'Well done lad!' he called. 'I have seen many a warrior become meat for the ravens. But now the curse is lifted and every Gutland war-dog shall praise you for all of your days.'

With that the banging began again, only this time it went on longer and it was twice as loud. It only stopped when a table collapsed behind me.

'Silence!' ordered King Ruffgar. 'It is our custom to hear the warrior himself tell his glorious tale. Sit you lot!' he commanded, and every war-dog sat obediently. Now there was total silence in the hall. 'Beowuff,' he continued, 'let's be having the details of your triumph over that Cursed Hen. Tell it blow by blow! Begin your battle-tale and don't spare the bloody details.'

Before I could start, Greytongue the Skald leapt up and spoke:

'Mighty Lord Ruffgar, before he speaks I must point out that we are missing one thing.'

'Awwww! I cannot abide a story-killer!' moaned Ruffgar in a fury. 'What in Bearded Bodin's name is missing? There is nowt missing!'

'My Lord, you who have seen the blood of so many fallen warriors burst forth from their bodies.'

'Aye old rhymer, what of it?'

'Where is the blood of Hendel? Where has the gore of the fowl-fiend gone? Not one speck adorns the walls of mighty Heorut hall.'

And with that the war-dogs gasped and turned to look at the walls. They were still as clean as the day they'd been painted, without a single splash of red.

'Beowuff!!' thundered Ruffgar, 'where's the wall-gore? Greytongue is right. There's always wall-gore whenever Hendel has been here to roost!'

Ruffgar's pack took up the cry of 'wall-gore' and my mind scrabbled like a rat in a barrel as I struggled to think of an explanation for them.

Then, once again, Ruffgar called for silence.

'Well Beowuff?' he thundered.

Just then, a voice called from the throng.

'Beowuff doesn't hack with a sword like other heroes.

He only uses paws, jaws and claws, remember?'

Arnuf spoke up for me like a true friend. He seemed to have forgotten that twenty minutes ago, I'd forbidden him to speak for a month. I could have jumped up and licked him on the nose!

But then the tongue-wagging Skald spoke again.

'You seem to know a lot about what happened last night, Arnuf. Perhaps you and this braggart Beowuff could demonstrate exactly how Hendel was slain without any blood being spilt?'

'Gladly!' I replied in an injured tone. 'Arnuf and I will show you exactly what happened.' 'We'll begin right now,' I said, assuming a heroic pose.

'Wait!' said Arnuf. 'Do you want me to play the part of you, or the monster?'

This drew laughter from the hall.

'I shall play myself,' I said wearily, 'and you, Arnuf, will play the part of our foe, the deadly hen-fiend.'

Now this was a stroke of luck. I could surely buy some time and entertain the pack by chasing Arnuf round the hall.

'Stand there on the bench Arnuf, and squawk in the manner of the red-feathered death-pecker,' I ordered.

'Wait!' barked the Skald at the top of his voice. 'Hendel was a flesh-tearing brute. Arnuf is far too timid for the role.'

Some of the carls began to snigger.

'Why don't you pick a real battle-hound to demonstrate what you did to that accursed bird,' demanded the Skald.

'Arnuf is a battle-hound,' I replied.

'He's a leak-leg,' howled a voice.

'Fair point,' said King Ruffgar. 'Come on then. Step forward, you blood-lappers! Who wants to play the monster in our midst?'

Of course, this sent the entire hall into a frenzy of shouting, barking and bench-banging once again.

As I stood and waited for this racket to die down, my inflated innards gave another horrid twist. For it was past sundown and I was due another dose of healing potion. I shifted from one leg to another, trying to find some relief.

As the baying died down, King Ruffgar inspected the crowd of young heroes who had stepped forward to play the hen-fiend.

'It's very nice to see so many thanes step up for glory in death and battle,' said the King. 'Can we have more than one monster?' he asked, turning to me. The pack of thanes howled in excitement.

My gut-sack almost split in fright! Before the Skald could talk me into more trouble, I shook my head sadly.

'Sorry bench-mates!' I sighed. 'But it doesn't do for a hero to exaggerate his deeds.'

'Pity!' said Ruffgar. 'I shall choose just one monster then. You!' he snapped, pointing into the midst of the pack. 'You can have the honour of playing the part of Hendel. You are indeed a right brute in war.'

The crowd in the hall immediately started bellowing the name: 'Pawstein! Pawstein!'

There he stood, licking his filed fangs. Then he began to circle me. He was carrying his favourite weapon: an axe with a blade the size of my head.

Pawstein was worse than Hendel. How was I going to convince him to let me pretend to slaughter him and please this gore-thirsty battle-pack?

As all the hall cheered for the popular Pawstein, a lone voice piped up from the crowd.

'Paws, jaws and claws! Just watch, that's all he needs!'

Ignoring this endorsement from Arnuf, and still squirming with pain from my rapidly inflating belly, I barged through the throng towards King Ruffgar.

'Dread Lord,' I explained, 'at this point in the struggle, Hendel was cowering from my war-cries. They were so loud that I soon had him clucking like a coward.'

'What of it?' asked Ruffgar.

'Please can you make Pawstein cower in that corner over there and cluck? This is a re-enactment after all.'

'Nonsense!' growled Ruffgar. 'Scare the beggar your-self if you want to get him clucking.'

Annoyed with my suggestion, the King began to shout for Pawstein and urge him onwards.

I looked at Ruffgar. He and Pawstein were whelps from the same litter all right. Their breed rule the meat-halls of this world. That is why I know that I cannot believe in the great Gnor and his kin, or Bodin the Bonefather or the rest of them. Where are the gods of the little dogs? What ill fortune, to be doomed to live in fear of bullying brutes like them.

I trembled, heart-in-maw as Pawstein came towards me, swinging the cleaver. I leapt aside as he brought it down with a blow which split a table in two. The whole hall laughed, except me.

Knowing full well that it was of little use, I tried to reason with Pawstein.

'Bench-mate!' I called. 'Hendel didn't have an axe, so can you put that chopper down?'

'I'll put it down all right!' he laughed. 'Where shall I split him lads?'

He lifted it high above his head and swung at me again. I fled like a fox from the pack but unfortunately, he caught the bottom of my cloak and pinned it to the floor with his vicious blade. Before he could strike again, I managed to jerk free and I danced away leaving that meat-head chewing a strip of my cloak.

The force of his blow was such that a large crack appeared in Heorut's ancient boards and spread slowly down the length of the floor. All the chanting and the banging and the brutish shouts of the war-dogs stopped. No-one in the hall knew where to look – at Pawstein, at me, at King Ruffgar or at the crack in his precious floor.

'Pawstein!' bawled Ruffgar, 'Leave my floor in one piece you hacking beggar! That's fine Gnorwegian ash that is. Mind you don't mark me hardwood when you chop down Beowuff!'

'Lord Ruffgar!' I pleaded, 'this is not how it was with Hendel. The feathered fiend did not have a weapon.'

But Pawstein was already charging at me with his iron-tipped paws flailing and his blood-axe swinging.

It is said that there are moments in battle where a hero has the chance to prove his mettle. The charge of this bruiser was one such moment. Would I rise to the challenge and face up to Pawstein's death-rush like a true whelp of war? Needless to say, I bravely bolted in the opposite direction.

Unfortunately, it meant bounding onto the royal table at the head of the hall and then leaping over Ruffgar and Queen Ethelpelt.

Pawstein couldn't resist the chase but he was twice as heavy as me and as he lunged at my throat, he knocked Muzzleguzzler out of Ruffgar's paw.

I chased down to the far side of the hall, dodging the King's thanes, with Pawstein snarling behind me. I was just about to gain the safety of the door when I was betrayed! Some trickster stuck a leg out and sent me flying. I rolled over and kissed the hardwood floorboards.

I cannot say for sure which evil little cat-licker tripped me up but the very next instant, that beast Pawstein was on me with a single bound.

I did my best to shield myself but he was both strong and vicious. He tore at my neck and throat with his iron-tipped claws and I am sure that if I hadn't been wearing the chain that the Irish Captain had put round me I would have been ripped to pieces and the King's hardwood floor would have had a coat of crimson varnish.

I could feel his cruel paws rake the fur down my back and draw blood at every rip. I tried to fight back but it was hopeless. As he was about to make the final death-bite at my neck, I barked at the top of my voice:

'Wait! You'd better not bite me Pawstein!'

'Why not, whelk-warrior?'

'Because you'll die of the Curse,' I growled.

'What do you mean?' he snapped, tilting his foaming mouth. 'I fear no curse from dog or god.'

'But this is the Curse of the Feathered-Fiend. I would hate for you to bite me and die of Hendel's witchcraft.'

At once, Heorut hall grew quiet. Then I saw King Ruffgar step forward.

'Let me finish this lying filth,' pleaded Pawstein, as the drool dripped from his jaws.

'Let him go, Pawstein,' ordered Ruffgar.

The King gestured with his battle-scarred paws for Pawstein to release me. I struggled up and tried to stand proudly in front of Ruffgar's assembled thanes, although I looked a sorry sight – for I was bruised and bleeding and I had been beaten like a common cur.

Slowly I took off my cloak and undid my tunic to display the effects of the Curse to the dumbstruck crowd.

I heard their whispers and cries of amazement.

'I have taken the Curse of Hendel upon myself. His magic is visible for all to see. My bloated belly is the witch-mark. Look! Feast your eyes on the wounded hero who brought this on himself to save Heorut and the dogs of Gutland and Ruffgar's kin.'

I paused as I turned to show them my swollen gut-sack. 'I have rid you of the hen-fiend. And this is how I am repaid. Humiliated in front of you. Bested in THIS CURSED STATE by a hale and hearty warrior. I have defeated Hendel and now you want to drag me from my sick-bed and beat me.'

It wasn't really a question but they began to shout loudly, 'NO…NO…NO' in unison.

Quickly, King Ruffgar called for calm.

'Beowuff lad, we owe you our thanks. You should have told me you were too sick for battle. Pawstein could easily have bitten you and then I'd have two cursed warriors.'

To my delight, Ruffgar demanded that I was placed near the royal table and they found me a straw-filled cushion which of course I accepted gratefully.

Just as I was about to relax, the Skald started bleating on again in a voice like a strangled goat.

'My Lord Ruffgar, we are all agreed that this Beowuff has brought great injury to himself on our behalf. But we have yet to hear the details of the death of Hendel and we need answers to our many questions. He owes us the story of his great deeds.'

'Wise words, Greytongue,' said Ruffgar, who was always desperately in need of entertainment. 'Tell us brave Beowuff, of the death of Hendel.'

'Well, Mighty Lord and Great Skald and Hounds of Gutland, although my throat aches for meat-mead and my bloated body cries for rest, I will tell the tale as best I can, then you shall feed the hall and me as well!'

At these words a cheer went up.

I had just enough strength left in me to tell them a tale they'd never forget.

'Night fell dismally and I waited with secret traps to catch the hen-fiend and end its days. Long, I waited until in the darkest hour when the whole world sleeps I heard a tiny scratch at the topmost window of Heorut. By means of stealth I opened the window to allow the shadow-stalker in. I hid in the dark and saw the night-shape approach. In came first one huge claw and then a mite-infested thigh and then the second great claw and then a second scaly thigh followed by its powerful, beastly wings. I knew that I had to hasten and so without fear I grabbed both its wart-encrusted legs and in one fell swoop I tied them together and the hen-fiend was held helpless! But just as I was about to secure the final knot, I felt the spear of the shadow-stalker's steely beak pecking at my throat. We grappled for an hour or more, evenly matched in strength, backwards and forwards across the floor of Heorut and I heard Hendel cry that never in all its hatched days had it faced a foe so mighty. For it had met its match in this dread hour. I did not weaken and neither did Hendel. But as I have only paws, jaws and claws to fight with so this horrid creature had beak, wings and talons twice as strong as mine. I knew that I must hold out till dawn for as the sagas tell, when day breaks through the cloud-murk and morning chases away the shadows of the night, a witch is at its weakest. When at last I felt Hendel's grip weaken and pull away, I knew I didn't have long. As soon as it saw the first streaks of light appear at the edge of the world, Hendel made one last strike at my snout. Still I did not flinch. As it tried to flap out through the window, I leapt up and grabbed one of its scaly legs and tore at it with all my might. But the hen-witch is a very strong creature Lord. To my shame, I could not manage a whole chicken's leg with my maw, so instead with both my paws I crushed its thigh bone in at least two places. White bone ends peaked from its leg-stump and it let out an awful squawk as it squeezed its broken body through the topmost window of Heorut hall. In its torment, it flapped off to its wicked roost.

So Gutlanders, Skald and King, that is why there is no wall-gore. That is why I am cursed, but even if I must die of a bloated belly, I can die knowing that I've rid your hall of the feathered death-pecker! For after the wound I inflicted, it cannot be long before the hideous hen flaps off to drown in some forsaken fen.'

When I had finished the saga, the hall fell silent. My eyes met Arnuf's through the gloom.

'And Arnuf was there to see it all,' said the weasel-tongued Skald. 'Is that right Arnuf?'

But before he could answer, Ruffgar spoke.

'Beowuff,' he said gravely, 'Do me one last favour.'

'Name it, my Lord. If my hen-pecked frame and egg-bound guts can grant it, it is yours,' I moaned.

'Stay one more night and finish it off if it returns.'

The hall rose as one and howled out their cheers.

'If it is King Ruffgar's wish, I say, aye!' I sighed.

'I thank you!' barked Ruffgar gruffly.

'Your bravery will fill our sagas for a thousand winters,' smiled the Skald.

'That's enough for tonight,' ordered Ruffgar. 'Beowuff, come with me to the Royal Kennel.'

The King regally dismissed his retainers and I limped behind him through the back door of the hall with the Queen and Arnuf in tow.

'Have you any requests for your second night, my hero?' asked the Queen when we were seated in their private chamber.

'He'll need more gold. And he'll probably want more meaty morsels again,' said Arnuf excitedly.

'Of course, anything else?' enquired the Queen.

'Strong rope,' I replied.

'Fair do's,' said the King. 'Is that it?'

'One more favour,' I said. 'A chariot.'

'A chariot?' exclaimed the Queen in surprise.

'You do use war-chariots, don't you?' I asked.

'Why do you need a chariot?' growled the King in a voice that could have shattered a stone-giant. His hackles were up and he fixed me with a suspicious look.

'In case I need to chase the fiend when he flees from my attack,' I said, quickly.

'Oh, of course! Fine,' barked the King.

'Mighty Lord Ruffgar, your generosity flies like a snow goose over the surface of the world,' I said (wondering whether I was pushing him too far), 'but there is just one more boon that I must beg of you.'

'And what is that?' asked Ruffgar gruffly.

'I know that you value the safety of Heorut and your warriors and kin above all else. I am told you have in your possession a magic horn...,' I began sweetly.

'If you're asking to borrow Muzzleguzzler, the answer is no,' snapped Ruffgar.

'Dread King, we are on the verge of a great victory but we need the help of magic to rid the land of this horrid hen-fiend,' I said.

'No-one touches me horn,' growled Ruffgar.

'But Lord...' I began.

'The answer is still no,' said Ruffgar.

The Queen looked at her Lord, disapprovingly.

'No horns!' tutted the King, 'But you can borrow Witchcleaver. It's the heaviest blood-axe in my collection. I can't say fairer than that. Now be off with you!'

With that he ordered that the hall should be triple guarded for the night and waved us away.

As we trotted back from the royal chambers, Arnuf could tell I was annoyed.

'Why is the horn so important?' he asked.

'Why do you think?' I sighed.

'Is it because it's covered in magic runes and it never needs filling up?' he asked.

'No,' I muttered, clutching at my belly. 'But it might have something to do with the fact that it's made of solid gold.'

'Will that help us defeat Hendel?' he asked.

'Alas no,' I sighed. For I had already made up a mountain of nonsense today, and I was fast running out of drivel. However, for my plan to work, I had to give Arnuf a good reason for needing Muzzleguzzler. So I dug deep and began to spout more lies: 'If we fill the horn up with this, we may be victorious.'

I reached into my bag and pulled out the white packet that the so called 'Hound of Healing' had given me.

'Remember this?' I said. 'This is deadly Hensbane. One sip would kill a grown dog, but a whole horn full of the stuff will kill anything. It might even make Hendel burst into flames! That's why we need the King's magic horn,' I explained. As usual, Arnuf lapped up my nonsense like meat-mead.

'Of course!' yapped Arnuf as he sniffed excitedly at the packet. 'It's just like the Hound of Healing said. If you're a hen, Hensbane is double-deadly.'

'Aye,' I said nodding. 'Exactly!'

'Fancy a taste?' he asked, offering me the packet.

'Stop Arnuf! You dozy doorstop!' I cried snatching it from his paw. 'It's still "single deadly" if you're a dog.'

Chapter Nine

Skaldduggery

So for a second night, I found myself alone in the King's meat-hall. I say 'alone in the hall' since I do not count Arnuf. He is as war-shy as I am myself and would be useless in a battle against the hook-beaked enchanter that now stalked my thoughts.

Well, bench-mates, since I have sworn to your cruel Lord to be a truth-sayer who will tell no word of a lie during this tale, I will answer your questions.

'Did you really fear that Hendel would attack?' you ask.

After my first night in the hall, I could remember very little. I could only think about my poor guts, which swung about like a Swede on a Gnorwegian gibbet.

Of course, that did not stop me from giving King Ruffgar and his thanes a good account of my victory over the dreaded beast. Too fine a tale perhaps – about the hen-fiend and its tearing talons and its steely beak and the flinty-white bone ends jutting from its splintered leg-stump. It all sounded most convincing and in short, I had scared myself witless. The idea that the feathered-menace might come flapping down the smoke-hole for a rematch turned my knees to marrow-jelly. The faces of Ruffgar's thanes did not help – they all shrank away from me as if I was an exiled cur.

The beating that Pawstein had given me

troubled me greatly; it felt like angry gnomes were driving heated spears into my flesh.

What is it about these thug-dogs that they seem to feel no pain? They limp back from war three-legged and idle away their homecoming night at the meat-bench without even feeling peaky. It is only when they try to stagger up from the table that they remember they have a leg missing!

Whimpering as I licked my wounds, I cursed the Bonefather for making me feel injuries so keenly.

The hours dragged as I lay by the fire-pit, willing the smoke-serpents to coil up to the rafters. As the long-fire burned down to its last embers, what courage I had died with the flames.

My bravery would have been completely extinguished were it not for the one thing that kept me in the hall – Muzzleguzzler. In my mind's green-eye, I'd already strung that golden beauty to my belt. How I longed to snatch it and bolt through the woods and be away and free! But King Ruffgar was no dolt, he had left his hall thrice-guarded. Alas, I had no clue where the horn was kept. Old Ruffgar probably tucked it under his snout at night and dribbled over it.

There was no meat-mead left, Arnuf had slobbered down the last of it. So I decided to drink some more of the potion that the so-called 'Hound of Healing' had given me.

There was nothing to do but lie down, out-stare the dying fire and wait for my doom.

I awoke to an eerie squawking that sent me scuttling

under the bench like a frightened sand-rat.

It was dark in Ruffgar's hall; not the half-darkness of a summer night, but mine-shaft black. I could not even see the end of my own snout. True to his words, the King had sealed the hall and there was not even a glimmer from the door-cracks to guide my way.

The fire was dead and an eerie chill had crept into Heorut. Poking my nose out from under the bench I peered into the darkness, but I could not make out anything. For a moment I thought I'd left the hall and been dragged to the lair of the night-dragon who feasts on the light. Squinting into the gloom, I saw a shape. It was some moments before I recognised it as the white tip at the end of Arnuf's tail. That muddle-minded mead-hog had swilled a gutfull and now he lay passed out on the boards – not even an ice-giant could rouse him from his slumber.

When the squawking came for a second time, it stopped my heart. A powerful scent was in my nostrils – the stench of witchcraft! I commanded my spell-bound legs to move; hauled myself out from under the bench and inched forward into the dark.

Was it finally come? The hour that the sagas tell of – when every pup must at last became a war-dog, or die trying? Alas bench mates, that hour will never come for old Beowuffer, not whilst I have any strength left in my legs to flee.

I sprang up and away towards the door, but to my horror – I soon realised that I had set off in the wrong direction.

I swivelled around, sniffing the air, trying to retrace my steps, until at last I found myself by the fire-pit. There I stood, under the smoke hole. A shaft of moonlight broke through the clouds and shone into the hall.

What did I see? What night-mare had bolted from the paddock of my dreams? The horrid-hen! The monster Hendel was before me, squawking and tearing at the boards with claws like meat-cleavers. I swayed like a young pine, whimpering at the sight of the fiend's steely beak, its dreaded talons and its unusually large head.

Few chickens are ever called pretty (save for the occasional house-pet clucked over by a Swedish grandmother). But if there was a competition for hens of a hideous appearance, this witch-spawn would win first prize.

The features of its face were chicken-like, but they were disfigured and twisted. It was as if the thing had been forged by a careless smith with a faulty furnace. Strangest of all, its eyes were covered by a leather hood.

Alas! The hen-fiend did not need to see me in order to hunt. It reared up and flapped, searching for my flesh with its claws and renting the air with its twisted beak.

I fumbled to free Witchcleaver, the axe that Ruffgar had loaned me, from my belt.

Back at home, my axe never saw action. In fact, I once spent a whole afternoon hacking at some oaks in order to make its blade look authentically battle-worn. If you ever need to fight a tree-army, I'm your war-dog, but I have no idea how to weild an axe in battle.

Witchcleaver was a war-notched old skull-splitter, but the accursed thing wouldn't unclip from my belt. What use is a warrior who can't unbuckle his own blood-axe?

I let out a terrible wail for help, and a shaky voice answered my call.

'Beowuff! Beowuff! Hendel is upon us!' cried Arnuf. 'Fear not, for I will stand shoulder-to-shoulder with you!'

'Thank you sheild-pal!' I cried with relief. 'The Skalds will sing sagas about your courage.'

There was a long pause.

'Er, where exactly are you?' he added.

'I'm over here!' I howled. 'Make haste Arnuf! Before I am pecked into slivers!'

I cried loudly for help and made appeals to various gods as I fumbled to untie the great axe. At last, I managed to untangle it.

With a war-cry that sounded more like a whimper, I raised Witchcleaver and swung it wildly at the fiend. Hendel squawked and let out an evil croak. Then it lunged at me, spearing the air with its vicious beak. Struggling to wield Ruffgar's mighty axe, at last I managed a swing and brought it down with a crash. There was the clang of metal on metal and a couple of the hen-fiend's steely claws were severed clean off.

Although I had struck off two of Hendel's talons, the witch-fowl did not shriek with pain, in fact it made no noise at all. Instead, it was I who gave out a wail.

'Arnuf!' I cried. 'To me! To me!'

I swung the axe again and again, but I could not land another blow on the fiend.

'Don't worry bench-mate, I will stand by you,' came a call.

At last, a figure appeared in the gloom at my side.

'Thanks!' I cried. 'But it would be better if you could stand in front of me,' and I gave him a firm shove in the back that sent him flying towards Hendel.

I heard a roar of rage and a string of curses. It was not Arnuf who had joined me, but Greytongue the Skald. My eager push had carried him to within pecking distance of the brute's beak, but he did not seem too worried. On his right paw, he wore a leather gauntlet.

He stumbled towards the winged-terror, raised his glove and whistled. Then he leapt up, and pulled off the monster's leather hood, revealing a pair of glowering yellow eyes like twin leak-holes in the snow.

'Hunt!' barked the old rogue in a voice like death.

As the feathered fiend flapped up to the rafters, I saw that it was held by a leash, attached to its foot. I dived for the safety of a table, but before I could reach it, there was a rush of wind and an awful swooshing and the thing had swooped down and seized me by the collar, and now it was lifting me howling up to the roof. As I rose into the air, I screamed and begged Arnuf to save me.

I cannot say for sure what the fowl-fiend had planned; perhaps it wanted to fly me back to its lonely lair and peck strips off me at its leisure? Or maybe it meant to drop me onto a rock, split my skull-case and gobble up my brains for its breakfast.

But it hadn't reckoned on my bloated belly! My gut-sack was wedged in the smoke-hole like a pup down a rabbit hole. I scratched at the wooden roof in terror, protecting my face with the blade of my axe.

'Curse you Skald!' I cried. 'Help! Call it off! Or...'

'Or what?' he laughed.

'Or I will tell King Ruffgar how you've been robbing him each time a hero comes to the hall.'

'That will be a tricky tale to tell,' snarled the Skald, 'after my winged beauty has torn out your tongue.'

'Rise!' he ordered, and the bird-fiend flapped twice as hard, trying to drag me out through the smoke-hole.

Before it could uncork me, I grabbed its leather leash with both paws. Squawking, it let me go and I crashed down and landed on top of the Skald with a thump. There was a satisfying crack as his muzzle hit the bench.

The Icelander was old in years but he was a sinewy brute and strong with it. He was dazed, but he soon got up again – and I sprang away from him in a panic.

'There you are! I've been looking for you,' panted a familiar voice. My blundering bench-mate had finally sniffed me out.

'Look Arnuf! See the traitor in our midst!' I howled, pointing an accusing paw at the Skald. 'That old cut-purse is in league with the hen-fiend. He's been using it to kill the heroes and steal the King's treasure.'

'Not old Greytongue?' said Arnuf, in wonder.

'Who do you believe Arnuf?' asked the Skald. 'This liar, a stranger who you have only known for two days, or me, your old friend and teacher.'

'He is the liar Arnuf,' I cried. 'Look! He has the feathered-devil on a leash. I'll run now and call Ruffgar's retainers. Guard him well Arnuf!'

'Guard him? From the hen you mean?' asked my bewildered bench-mate.

'No Arnuf!' I moaned.

Getting Arnuf to understand this was likely to prove worse torture than being beaked by the hen-fiend itself. 'I mean guard that worm-worded traitor over there. Do not let him escape.'

'Hunt!' cried the old Icelander, and he let out a shrill whistle and held his gauntlet high in the air.

With a fearsome squawk, the beast swooped back through the smoke-hole and hurtled down towards us extending its steel-edged talons.

As I dived under the table again, I saw that Arnuf did not move a muscle. He just twisted his snout and smiled at the beast. For the second time, and not for the last, I felt sorry for him. He had the wits of a pickled herring but he didn't deserve to be de-boned and pecked into strips by the hen-fiend.

Arnuf greeted the monster with a laugh.

'It's Longflapper!' he called in a sing-song howl 'Hello! Who's a beautiful hawk?'

To my amazement, the creature checked its dive and landed with a crash at his side.

It eyed him, as if it were in two cruel minds about whether or not to strike.

I could see the monster's thoughts in motion. Part of it wanted to cleave the weak-wit's skull in two, but behind its beady eyes, some dim memory of kindness held it back.

'Run Arnuf!' I cried. 'That's not Longflapper, that's Hendel!'

'No!' crooned Arnuf. 'He's not a monster! He's a just very long flapper!'

Stunned, I saw that the Arnuf was right! Before us stood Longflapper, the King's war-hawk, although it had been decked out in a hideous mask, and it had somehow grown claws of iron.

The Skald and I watched in wonder, waiting to see what the dreaded death-pecker would do next. And for once I did something slightly brave. Rather than rushing from the hall, I seized the gauntlet from the Skald in my teeth and made off with it. For I knew that hunting hawks are trained with a leather glove and taught never to attack the glove-wearer.

The grey-muzzled rhymer began to whimper.

'Give it back!' he cried. 'Quick! Before he pecks me to pieces!'

The bird looked from Arnuf to the Skald and then to me, twisting its head towards the glove to await my command.

'Tell your tale,' I ordered. 'And if I were you, I'd keep it brief and make sure that there are no Swedes in it.'

The bird glared at the Skald, scratched at the boards, and let out a little squawk.

'He says that when he's hunting,' observed Arnuf.

The Skald was soon talking. We heard about his taste for gaming, fine meats and the need to put away a large pile of gold for his old-age. When it was over, he added a sob-story about losing all his money to a crooked lender in his homeland.

'Never trust a banker from Icelandland!' sighed Arnuf.

'Quickly Arnuf!' I commanded. 'We have heard enough. Run and fetch the hall-guards!'

'Wait!' begged the Skald. 'Do not tell! I beg you! If King Ruffgar ever learns of this, he'll have scraps of my ears on every leaking post in Gutland.'

Holding the gauntlet up, I considered his case. The old Icelander was a proven liar and a thief, and a rotten-rhymer, but so was I. The only thing that set us apart from each other was the fact that he'd used his king's own hawk to kill scores of visiting heroes. This last offence is not quite as bad as it sounds – if you'd met as many heroes as old Beowuff, you'd know why.

'Give me one good reason why I shouldn't tell old Ruffgar exactly what you've been up to?' I asked.

'Muzzleguzzler!' he moaned, knowing my heart only too well. 'I know you want that golden horn! I have seen it in your eyes, but you'll never steal it without my help.'

CHAPTER TEN

BIG HORN HUNTING

The Skald and I made a bargain. I would have the golden horn and be on my merry way, and no word of his hero-slaying tricks would ever reach Ruffgar's ears (or to be more precise, Ruffgar's 'ear' – because one of them had been flayed from his royal head by a Dragon-raider's whip. A similar fate would await our ears, if he ever discovered our plot).

There was one problem with our little arrangement – by the name of Arnuf.

'Where are we going now?' he asked, as we walked slowly towards the north wall.

'Sssssh!' said the Skald. 'Be silent Arnuf!'

'We're after the real Hendel!' I explained. 'He may be close.'

As usual Arnuf gobbled up my half-stewed nonsense like jellied offal. So far, so good.

Twelve steps from the door, the Skald stopped in his tracks. The hunter's moon was high in the sky and its beams shone down through the cracks in the roof. I saw the old rhymer reach into his tunic and take out a woollen bag. He rummaged around inside it for a while until at last he pulled something out.

'What's that?' yapped Arnuf in excitement.

Silver metal glinted in the moon-beams. Taking it for a blade, I bared my teeth and stepped back.

'It's the key,' said the Skald. 'Move aside Arnuf, you are standing on the door.'

'I think you'll find that I am standing on the floor,' laughed Arnuf.

The Skald dragged him aside by the collar, and pressed the little key into a cranny in the floorboards. I heard a faint click, no louder than a snapping twig.

The cunning old Icelander lifted up a flap to reveal a flight of steps leading down into the dark.

'After you!' said the Skald, wagging his tail.

'Please – you go first!' I countered. Bodin himself could not drag me into that dark cave whilst the old murderer stood behind me with the key in his paw.

The Skald nodded and descended into the pit first.

'A tunnel!' yapped Arnuf. 'Does it lead down to Hendel's nest?'

As I climbed down the steps into that musty cave, I heard a crack as the timbers gave way beneath me.

'Ware ye! The boards are rotten,' warned the Skald.

'So much for Gnorwegian wood,' I said. 'And the King takes such pride in it too.'

'He would boast less if he knew the builders,' laughed the Skald. 'His whole hall is made of the cheapest pine that the land of the Swedes can offer.'

'Where does this filthy troll-hole lead to?' I asked, stepping over a pile of bones.

'It will bring us up in the corridor outside the Royal Chambers,' said the Skald. 'Go inside and you will see two war-chests. The prize you seek is kept inside the smaller one. And the very best of fortune to you!'

'Does it look as if my brain-case is cracked?' I growled. 'What kind of weak-wit do you take me for? You must come with me. We don't have a bargain until the golden horn is safe in my loot- sack.'

The Skald sniffed sadly. He knew that I had a point. Only a cast-iron fool would go creeping into Ruffgar's chamber leaving the other outside to raise the alarm and spin a story to the guards.

'Arnuf?' I called. 'We have a little task for you.'

Two minutes later the Skald and I stood on the threshold, our legs quivering and our ears cocked for any sign of trouble. There came a loud scrabbling from inside and then we heard the clatter of armour. For a terrible moment, I feared that my weak-witted pal had been discovered.

'I've got it!' cried Arnuf, crashing out of the door with a loot-sack in his maw.

'Thank Bodin the Bearded Bonefather!' I laughed. But my face fell when I opened the bag.

'What's this?' I thundered.

'A horn of mould, like you said,' whined Arnuf.

'Gold! Not mould! You feeble-witted fumbler,' I whispered, glowering at him.

'That's the squirrel-pot Arnuf,' sighed the Skald.

It is beyond my understanding. How could anyone mistake the magic horn Muzzleguzzler, (forged by the master smith Weyland himself) for a pewter pot filled with scrapings from the cage of the Queen's squirrel.

'Try again,' sighed the Skald, passing Arnuf the sack.

'There's no time,' I growled. 'Let us all go in there and finish this quest together.'

Before he could protest, I shoved the Skald through the open door and followed fast behind him.

The chamber was dark but there, by a wall-hanging depicting a bothered looking bear, were two wooden chests. The smallest one was unopened. Remembering the Skald's words, I rushed to it and tried the lid. It was locked and I growled at the Skald accusingly.

Noiselessly, he sneaked over to the wall-hanging. From behind the bothered bear's nose he drew out a tiny key. I snatched it from him and tried the lock.

There it was before me! The most delicately engraved, most wonderful golden drinking horn that I have ever cast my thieving eyes upon. In a flash, I cast my thieving paws on it and stuffed it into my loot sack.

At this moment, there was crash and a stirring and a great clamour. An angry voice began to bellow curses by the cartload.

'It's King Ruffgar!' cried the Skald. 'He's awake!'

'We are undone!' I moaned, hearing the swish of wall-hangings and the clack-clack-clack of iron-clad claws on the wooden boards. Gripped by terror, I did what any of you would do in these circumstances.

'Here! Take this and hide it!' I cried, throwing my loot-sack to Arnuf.

The Skald sprang up and caught it in his teeth, just

as Ruffgar strode into the chamber, kitted out in full battle-armour.

'What do you lot think you're doing?' he growled.

The Skald threw himself down at Ruffgar's feet.

'My Lord! My Lord –' he began.

'I know, I know. Murderoc Bloodsacker is attacking us,' said the King. 'But that doesn't give you the right to come barging in here.'

The King's eyes scoured the room and landed on the dark chest with its lid hanging open and its precious contents missing.

'Muzzleguzzler!!!' he cried, brandishing his axe. 'Give me back my horn! Or I'll have yer brains for war paint!'

'Excuse us Lord,' I said calmly. 'But we were waiting for Hendel in the hall, when we heard noises. Thinking it was the monster, we followed it.'

'Down a tunnel,' said Arnuf.

'Down a tunnel,' I sighed with relief. 'Which led us here to your chamber. And who do you think we caught key-in-paw, rummaging in your royal chest?'

'No! No! He lies my Lord!' whimpered the Skald, wailing and banging the boards in his torment.

'A horn-robbing Skald,' I sighed sadly. 'Who would have thought it! We moan about the young, but it's always the grey-muzzles that you have to be on guard for. Look under his tunic and you'll find he has a loot-sack.'

Ruffgar took a war-horn from the rack and blew a

loud blast on it. Then he turned to Arnuf.

'Seize him!' he ordered.

'Seize who Lord?' asked Arnuf.

'That treacherous Icelander of course,' said King Ruffgar, pointing at the Skald.

Queen Ethelpelt, who had heard the commotion, came trotting in with a pack of hall-guards at her tail. When she learned the sad story, she turned to Ruffgar with tears in her amber eyes.

'Greytongue has served us long my Lord. Show mercy – stay your paw and send him into exile.'

'Send him back to Icelandland,' suggested Arnuf. 'He'd like it there.'

'Silence!' roared the King, his bull-neck shaking with rage. 'There will be no exile.'

Then Ruffgar turned to Greytongue, who lay quivering in a heap, beating his paws against the boards in a display of regret.

'Listen to me old Skald' cried Ruffgar. 'I will have my vengance soon!'

'Er. How soon my Lord?' I asked. 'Is it not kinder when justice is served swiftly?'

'Not now,' said Ruffgar, giving me a strange look. 'I need him to do my battle speech, then my hunting hawk will tear out his lying tongue and feast upon it.'

And with that he took up his shield, his axe and his broadsword and strode off. Half way down the corridor he turned and barked a last instruction:

'Don't feed the hawk wife, I want to keep him hungry for Skald's tongue.'

CHAPTER ELEVEN

THE KING'S SPEECH

King Ruffgar fixed me with a stare that would scare a troll and let out a rasping growl.

'Well hero, 'there's no blood without slaughter,' as my dear old mother used to say. I might not have proof that you've been misbehaving, but consider yourself lucky that I don't string you up on a gibbet.'

I shuddered to hear this, and my bloated belly started to turn somersaults again.

'However, you're in luck, for I've run out of rope.'

'If it is rope that you seek, why not ask Threadweaver, the rope-maker Lord,' suggested Arnuf.

My bench-mate's flapping tongue would get some poor cur killed one day – and I was high up the list of candidates!

'Don't worry hero!' chuckled Ruffgar. 'I'm not in a hanging mood. In fact, I've got some news that will bring you good cheer...'

He left his sentence hanging and I dangled, waiting for his next words.

'You're going to war instead!' he laughed. 'With us! Against our sworn enemy – the hated Hackerfolk.'

He announced this as if the news that I was to be sent to battle a savage pack of blood-lappers was something I should be delighted about.

'The Hackerfolk?' I whined.

'That's right. We're going on a Hacker hunt – and you're coming too! Forget that Horrid Hen nonsense. This'll be the perfect chance to prove your courage in battle – the old fashioned way.'

My stomach knotted up at the thought of it.

'This 'un will be a proper ding-dong,' said Ruffgar, 'Old Murderoc's only gone and invaded us this time!'

So we set off down the road towards the Gutland shore; the King and I, and his willing war-dogs. As well as that pack of bruisers, I had Arnuf and the old Skald to keep me company. The latter bumped along at the rear in a specially made cage, throwing insults at his bearers – rhyming ones no doubt.

I couldn't understand why the King hadn't already finished off the loot-picking Icelander, but as I was to find out, Ruffgar had one more duty in mind for his Skald before the death sentence was carried out.

On the way to the beach, Arnuf told me more about our mutual foe, the Hackerfolk. I'd never heard of them before but I soon found out that the Hackers are a warlike breed (no surprises there then) who'd forsworn the land and lived on boats. Arnuf didn't actually use the word 'forsworn' but he was able to explain the concept by means of some leaves and a muddy puddle. His demonstration of how they never came ashore lasted all through our hearty breakfast.

'Never die on an empty stomach!' was apparently another saying of King Ruffgar's charming mother.

As I have said, I learned that the Hackers are a seafaring tribe who have vowed never to set paw on land. From what I'd seen of Gutland, I didn't blame them! I was thinking of making a similar vow myself.

The only exception to their 'no landing' rule is that they are allowed put ashore in order to wage war on inferior breeds. Fortunately, for the land-lovers amongst the Hackers, this is something that they do on a very regular basis.

After a day's march, we reached a stone-strewn stretch of beach. The war-dogs passed a number of messages about the camp, and we were all told to stay on the look out for Murderoc Bloodsacker, the King of the Hackerfolk. As we took up out positions, I was advised by Ruffgar to have my blood-axe ready for the Hacker King's neck at every opportunity, so I decided to find out what Arnuf knew about him.

'He's a famous Hacker warrior. His friends call him 'Murder' for short,' explained my beach-mate.

Well, as I am still sworn to tell no word of a lie, I must reveal that I had no intention of setting a paw anywhere near the enemy, especially not near an enemy named Murderoc.

Instead, I planned to loiter at King Ruffgar's side for as long as possible and then slip off with some excuse before things got nasty. In fact, I was already muttering something about needing to varnish the shields, when Murderoc's standard-bearer came trotting through the Gutland mist.

This Hacker was every inch a weird-eyed killer, with

hobbies including tail-biting as well as the usual looting and pillaging. It is no word of a lie to say that he made the worst of the Gutlander war-pack look like innocent lambs.

I did my best not to cower as he came striding up the stones, towards where Ruffgar's thanes had set up our battle standard.

The Gutlanders, however, did not seem in the least bit bothered to see this beast arrive. Some of them even nodded to him cheerily.

Now you might find it strange but in this land it was not unusual for two armies to meet and discuss the running order of the day before battle commenced.

Pawstein was chosen to speak on behalf of King Ruffgar, and he leapt forward and glared at the messenger in a suitably vicious manner. Then the two brutes began to negotiate, but the Hacker struggled with the language of Gutland. Pawstein himself spoke not a word of the Hacker tongue but he made himself understood by shouting very slowly.

'We'll let your lot land and form up your battle lines here on the beach,' he bawled.

'Hack! Beach!' replied the messenger.

Pawstein shook his head furiously.

'No hacking on the beach!' he growled. 'That's against the law here in Gutland.'

The Hacker looked disappointed.

'We'll line up over there by King Ruffgar's shield-fort.'

'Hack! Shield-fort!' howled the messenger.

'No!' growled Pawstein firmly. 'No hacking the King's shield fort. Not till battle's started, anyway.'

The messenger looked crestfallen as Pawstein continued.

'King Murderoc can have his shield-fort over there by the grey rocks.'

The messenger nodded in agreement. Pawstein nodded back at him and smiled, muttering something through his bared teeth.

'Right. Next we'll send out our champions to do battle. Single combat first,' explained Pawstein.

'Hack! Single-hack first!' barked the Hacker.

'That's right! Single hack first!' repeated Pawstein. It was like trying to explain the rules of Gutball to Arnuf.

'And when your champion lies dead on the sand, I'll give the signal to begin – we'll throw Bodin's Spear at your lot, so you'll know exactly when to start. The side who break through their enemies' shield-fort and capture their battle-standard will be the winners. Whoever wins the day can pillage, loot and scent-mark at will.'

'Hack?' barked the messenger.

'Oh never mind,' bawled King Ruffgar. 'Let's get on with it!'

The Hacker seemed to know that the parley was over, and he blew a long blast on his war horn. All of a sudden, the beach began to swarm with Hackerfolk as they disembarked from their longships and assembled in battle order.

As the Hacker messenger strode off towards the grey rocks, King Ruffgar could not resist a final word.

'Tell that beggar Murderoc that I want a proper bloody battle this time. And none of yer silly skirmishing mind!' he barked.

I noticed one of the Hackers carrying what looked like a leather bag on the end of a long stick.

'What's that?' I asked.

'A blood-bladder,' answered Arnuf.

'What's inside it?' I asked, already wishing I hadn't.

'Blood,' said Arnuf, before I could stop him.

Then I noticed many more sacks on poles waved by the Hackerfolk.

'They're mad about their bladders,' he explained. They drain the warm blood from their foes and squeeze it into those sacks. Then they stick them on the end of their poles.'

'What in the name the Bearded Bonefather do they do that for?'

'To take home to their families, as presents,' explained Arnuf.

'Who's that over there, with the biggest bladder?'

'That's Murderoc Bloodsacker. He's their King you know. He's not very well liked around here.'

This news came as no great surprise to me, but there was no time for more Gutland gossip because at that moment, King Ruffgar's shield-thanes wheeled Greytongue's cage into sight. The old Skald was in chains now and he seemed to have withered and shrunk like a two-week-old sausage.

'Before the two armies fight, it's time for the speeches,' said Arnuf. 'After Greytongue does our speech, King Ruffgar will cut off his tongue and feed it to Longflapper.'

'Will he?' I gasped in horror.

'Oh yes,' replied Arnuf. 'Longflapper loves tongues.'

I was surprised to learn that Hackers have their own tradition of Skalds and they had brought one of their high poets to perform a piece for King Murderoc before the battle.

Although it is true that I am war-shy, I do have something of a knack for languages, and I remember most of the poem in question, so I have recorded it here so that it will not be lost to history.

> *Hack! Hack! Hack!*
> *Hack! Hack! Hack!*
> *Hack! Hack! Hack!*
> *Hack! Hack! Hack!*
> *Hack!*

Throughout this performance, I noticed that the Hacker Skald kept looking at a strip of bark.

'That's got the pictures on it,' said Arnuf.

I twisted my head in bewilderment.

'The pictures! In case he forgets his lines,' he explained.

'Hark!' boomed a loud voice from somewhere near.

'Hack!' shouted the Hacker Skald, aggressively.

'No, Hark!' called Greytongue again, from inside his cage.

'No, Hack!' said Arnuf.

'Shut your muzzle Arnuf, Greytongue is about to speak,' I ordered.

'H-A-A-A-R-K!' howled the old Skald.

The whole beach fell silent.

Caged up like that, the Icelander looked like a criminal cur, but his rolling voice still commanded respect.

Hark, you wet-pawed sea-whelp,
Your bark is worse than your bite.
And your bark is worse than your verse.
And your wooden words.
Written on your bit of bark.
Would bore a beetle to death.
And Hark, you barking Hackers,
See what is stood before you –

Good Gutlanders, Ruffgar's guardians
Bladder-wrackers, Hacker-mockers
Come and speak with our
thin-lipped mocking axes!!

Ruffgar's thanes raised a massive cheer at these words and they started chanting the Good Gutlanders lines and banging their shields in unison. King Ruffgar looked pleased and went over and rattled the Skald's cage.

'Come on, old word-hound, give us more and prepare us for battle,' said Ruffgar. This request got a howl of approval from the war-dogs of Gutland.

I was hoping that after one more verse of this drivel they would get on with it so I could slink off and find a good hiding place.

Ruffgar's request seemed to send the Hacker-Skald into fits of rage and he started to shout:

'Hack! Hack! Hack!' even louder than before.

But Greytongue shook the bars of his cage so hard that he broke one of them and stuck his head out of the gap.

Oh, Hacker-Skald, go back to school
Learn somes rhymes and Bodin's rules
Or do what Hacker-folk do best
And hack off your own head instead!

The Hacker-Skald was no match for Greytongue and he did not understand the mockery.

'Hack?' said the Hacker-Skald fiercely.

Well, that was it. The whole of Ruffgar's army let out gales of laughter. Even Ruffgar, who took warfare seriously, let out a chuckle and slapped the shields of his war-pack.

For a brief moment I actually felt some sympathy for

the Hacker-Skald – then I remembered why they were called the Hackerfolk.

Amongst the howls of laughter and the clanking of axes on shields I heard cries of 'Set him free!! Let him go,' all begging Ruffgar to be merciful.

'Cut out his tongue! Cut out his tongue!' I called, trying to get a group of us shouting it. Alas, it was to no avail. The crowd and Ruffgar had all fallen for the Skald's mocking lines. It was what is known as a 'head-saver' of a poem – although in this case it was also a 'tongue-saver' because poor old Longflapper would have to go hungry tonight.

'Good old Greytongue. He's from Icelandland, you know,' called Arnuf.

The old word-weasel was imprisoned behind his wooden bars, but he was still ready to play one more trick on me.

'Shall I introduce your champion, my King?' he shouted.

'What champion?' growled Ruffgar.

'For the single combat Lord,' explained the Skald. 'Thanes of Gutland, I give you The Slayer of Hens, The Menace of Mangefeld. Giantesses cower at his bark and white-fanged water-worms wet themselves when he approaches...'

'Who?' barked Ruffgar. 'Who are you pointing at?'

'Beowuff!' shouted the Skald, nearly blue in the face.

'Oh very good! Why didn't I think of that? Bring the

hero to me,' said Ruffgar to two of his shield-thanes.

They were already over-excited and I was dragged before the mighty King of Gutland.

Ruffgar went straight to the point.

'Now listen here hero, it's very simple. See that great muck-sniffing clod over there?'

Ruffgar stuck out a paw and pointed at a dog the size of a barn. 'Him over there,' said Ruffgar, 'the one with no helmet on.'

I wondered why my enemy wasn't wearing a helmet, but I did not dare to ask.

'That great big 'un, armed with the stone on a pole,' added the King, pointing at my foe with his iron-clad paw.

'I see him,' I gasped. He had fists like feasting benches.

'That's him! He's Murderoc's youngest brother. Slainpile's his name,' said Ruffgar.

'Aye,' said a voice at my side, 'they call him Slainpile Stone-pole.'

'Do they call him that because he's as tall as a pole and as hard as stone?' I asked.

'No,' said the voice. 'They call him that because he's got a stone on a pole. No-one ever gets near him!'

I suddenly felt queasy and patted my bloated belly.

'I fear I'm still sick from the curse of Hendel my Lord,' I said.

At this stage I was trying to plead without making it sound like I was actually begging not to be sent to my death.

'Nonsense,' boomed the King, 'I want you to trot over there and bash his bloomin' head off.'

Every dog in the circle of thanes who made up Ruffgar's shield-fort began to cheer.

'Don't worry, hero, we won't start the battle till you've defeated him.'

'Thanks,' I moaned.

'Mind out though lad,' warned King Ruffgar, 'he's hard for a Hacker.'

Before I could make an excuse, the Skald smiled and clenched his paw in a salute to all the dogs of war who stood around him.

'Bench-mates!' he cried, 'Gutlanders! Shield-pals! Please move your tails and give an almighty cheer for your King's champion – Beowuff the Bear-hearted!!'

'Beowuff! Beowuff for Gutland!' came the chant.

I felt more wretched than ever before. Here I was being cheered on by hordes of Gutlanders in front of the most fearsome army for a hundred leagues. All I wanted to do was to sit quietly down in front of a roaring fire with a bowl full of meat-mead. Instead I was about to face certain death on the end of an enormous pole. The mad cheering of the Gutlanders only made me feel worse.

I trotted down the grim beach in-between the two great armies. In all the confusion, I realised that I'd forgotten my armour.

'Hack! Hack! Hack!' came the predictable shouts

from the enemy lines, although their faces were not visible – a sea-fret had descended and shrouded the beach in mist.

I heard a cry from behind me:

'Paws, jaws and claws! Paws, jaws and claws!'

How can four small words change a dog's life so much? Why did I ever tell Arnuf anything at all about anything?

All I could see of the enemy's lines were a few blood bladders on poles swinging gently in the breeze. This really was the end, I thought. I was about to have my guts mashed and poured into a leather bladder.

These beasts looked as if they were good at the Arts of War, which in these parts included: spilling-blood, disembowelling the fallen and thwacking their foes with massive stones.

All I could do was hope the end would come swiftly and under the cover of the mist so that no-one would see me being slaughtered.

My tongue was dry with fear. I always go dry-mouthed into battle.

Such a curious thing is life. Here was I with a swollen belly, full of terror and wild imaginings and yet still so fiercely thirsty. I reached into my bag and found the potion that the Hound of Healing had given me.

Then I remembered the little white packet full of Hensbane and I gave it some serious thought. Hensbane was a deadly herb. If I took it, I might drift off into a lovely sleep.

But something stayed my paw, so instead I wolfed down my gut-medicine. It was cool and milky but it made me feel even more sick.

Suddenly, the mist lifted and the enemy were visible in all their terrifying glory.

Only a couple of hundred yards away in front of me, filling one of Gutland's dreary beaches with savage colour, were the armed ranks of Hackers.

There they stood, in battle formation. Some held aloft huge bladders filled with blood and others waved their blood-red spears at us. Strangest of all, they were all swaying in unison. Spellbound, I watched them move slowly to one side and then to the next and I, too, found myself swaying.

Behind them, their longships were tied together in a chain. On board, their females were tending huge, steaming pots of food, looking after their young and sharpening their gutting knives.

I stared into their ranks and then again at the bobbing boats and I realised that these sea-dogs had no land-legs. Even on dry land, they all swayed about as if they were still aboard their floating sea-halls.

It wasn't much bench-mates, but it was a weakness of sorts and your old friend Beowuff would need to try every trick in the book if he was going to defeat a Hacker giant with stone on a pole.

Chapter Twelve

Slainpile Stone-pole

As I made my way to the mid point between the two armies, I had a sudden thought. Facing Slainpile Stonepole ought to get me into an epic poem, at the very least.

I shouted over to the biggest of the bladder-holders:

'Oy, Stain-pile, I want a word with you.'

'Hack! Kill! Hack!' bawled Slainpile, roaring like a bated-bull.

I saw that he was absolutely enormous, and then he stood up properly. As he trotted towards me I felt the whole beach shake.

'Hey Stain-pile!' I yelled, in a warlike manner. 'Yes! you, you great blubber-brain!'

Slainpile took a couple of steps forward to give himself a little room in front of his own troops. Then he lifted an enormous pole as long as a ship's mast. Attached to the end was a fearsome rock on a chain.

Slainpile wasn't a dog to waste his words. He was probably struggling to remember the word 'hack' so he only grunted slightly as he brandished the weapon.

'Stain-pile!' I shouted again, to break the quiet. For I always find silence a bit eerie on a battlefield.

I heard the whir of the rock as Slainpile began to swing it around his head. I didn't hear a peep out of

King Ruffgar's ranks but the Hackerfolk waved their bladders in an unnerving fashion.

Slainpile started to do little tricks, tossing the rock around like a ball on a string.

I knew I must think fast before they named me Beowuff the Flat.

Then I tried a trick of my own that had been forming in my mind. I wanted to encourage the Hacker army to imagine they were in the midst of a storm. So I began to sway.

Slowly they responded and the swaying spread like a fever through their ranks. Some of the Hackerfolk now stood with legs planted wide apart to cope with this thing called solid ground.

'Oy, Stain-pile! The earth is moving!' I shouted. I pointed to his fellows behind him who were all now swaying wildly on dry land. He turned to look at them and instinctively began to sway himself. This affected his rhythm with the pole and he lost control of it and misjudged the flight of his stone. It crashed into the front rows and knocked the heads off at least ten of his own warriors. There was chaos in the ranks as many Hackers fled the next circuit of the stone.

A huge cry went up from Ruffgar's troops who started cheering my name.

As the dead and injured were carried from the front ranks, more Hackers stepped forth to fill their places. Slainpile was angry, having just made a big pile of slain warriors – but on the wrong side of the battle-lines.

'Hey Stain-pile!' I called. 'You're slaying the wrong side, you great kelp-breathed clod!'

Shield banged on shield and there were huge cheers and shouts in the name of Gutland. Even King Ruffgar bellowed with laughter.

Slainpile took up a fighting stance and began to size me up. I dashed mouse-footed about the beach, first to the left and then to the right and then back and forth, trying to tempt the dog with the log to strike a blow.

Slainpile raised his huge paws and with perfect control brought the stone smashing down on top of me. Except, I had moved. Not very far, admittedly. Sand showered into the air and I feared I'd been buried alive as I fought my way back to daylight.

The stone lay perfectly still. Slainpile thought he'd smashed me to bits until I appeared triumphantly out of my shallow grave and paraded before Ruffgar's pack. Once again they didn't let me down. I could feel the heat of battle-lust coming from the Gutlanders.

'Oy! Lame-pile! What's your king's name?'

Slainpile didn't answer.

'You must know him. He's your own brother,' I suggested, helpfully.

Slainpile spoke in a huge bellow: 'Murderoc! Hack!'

'Do you know what we Gutlanders call Murderoc?' I asked.

'Hack!' barked Slainpile.

I took that answer as a 'No'.

'Murderoc the Mange-Pelted. Murderoc the Meat-

Head. Murderoc the Mound-Sniffer.'

I shouted this at the top of my lungs for all to hear.

The laughter began again, along with war-cries from King Ruffgar's pack. The Hackerfolk responded by waving their blood-bladders. Carnage was imminent.

Slainpile hauled the pole out of the crater and began to whirl the rock around his head again. I had one more trick left. If I could make a run at Slainpile's legs whilst he was swinging his stone I might encourage Ruffgar's troops to join me in attacking him.

So I charged towards Slainpile at full pelt. Alas, all the terror and exertion was playing havoc with my swollen gut-sack. The meaty longship which was still beached in my belly was beginning to rise on the tide. I was forced to stop for a breather well before I got anywhere near Slainpile.

Was the cat fight in my stomach due to nerves? Or was the 'curse' of Hendel taking its course? My gut swelled to enormous proportions and ripped the brooch from my tunic. I fell quivering onto the dank sand.

Slainpile laughed as he swung his stone around his head, aiming it accurately.

I waited, shaking.

Then, in the names of Bodin, Gnor, and my dear mother Mingingfrith, what I am about to tell you is the truth of all truths.

Between the ranks of armed warriors intent on battle and on Gutland's dreariest beach; the loudest, fiercest, most powerful, longest, crow-scaring emission of wind passed like a hurricane from out of my belly, under my cloak and out over the sea-misted shores. The windy report from my behind was heard by every iron-clad warrior, female and pup on the Hackerfolk's ships. I'll bet that even the servants in the hall of Heorut heard it.

I fell down exhausted and deflated, giddy with relief but barely able to move.

At first the shock of my explosion left the warriors mystified but as word passed down the ranks about of the source of the smell, the Gutlanders fell into such laughter that nothing could be heard above the din.

This was too much for Slainpile. No-one had ever mocked him and lived. He spun his stone around so fast that the earth shook and the sea began to rise, sending large waves crashing towards the shore. He screwed up his face and his eyes buckled out of their sockets. It was like watching a sausage splitting open on a cook-fire.

But Slainpile was in trouble. He'd been swinging with such speed and ferocity that the chain was coming loose. Now he was about to become the final victim on his own pile of slain hounds. The chain gave way, the deadly rock changed direction and it fell jerking towards his head.

There came a thick thud that made every warrior on the battlefield groan: Slainpile had been stoned by his own pole. Toppling like a felled oak, he crashed to the ground, crushing the breath out of a score or more of Hacker warriors.

Taking this as my cue to flee, I got up, brushed the sand from my coat and set off down the beach at full pelt. Ruffgar's pack took this as the signal to charge at the enemy.

'Gutland! Ruffgar!' was the battle cry of the charging war-hounds.

'And Beowuff!' I cried to myself, glad that I still lived. Whether any of the rest of Ruffgar's pack chanted my name, I cannot say.

I had no intention of doing any more fighting, so I turned to watch as the opposing ranks of war-dogs tore into each other. The clash of iron on iron, wood on wood and the howls of the wounded and the dying soon filled my ears.

It is impossible to describe the heat of battle between two armies ready to fight to the death at close quarters. I stood and trembled.

I fear that the battle did not go off as it does in the sagas. For brave King Ruffgar's charge soon turned into a rout. All around him the shields were falling as one by one the Hackerfolk set about their murderous work. Gutland's heroes fell on the reddened sand and I could only watch as Ruffgar was surrounded by a screaming mob.

'Hack! Hack!' came the blood-curdling cries, until the poor King stood alone.

Then, at last Murderoc himself stepped forward. He was big, but only half the size of his late brother, Slainpile. He struck a fearsome blow at Ruffgar which connected below the fore-paw. Desperately, the Gutland King fought on until the fray drifted over to where I was cowering (behind a seaweed-covered boulder).

'Beowuff! Thank the Bonefather you're here,' called Ruffgar. 'Throw me an axe and I will fight this begger one-pawed!'

Murderoc looked around in confusion, wondering why his foe was talking to a rock.

Did I stir from my hiding-place? Not old Beowuffer.

'Quick Beowuff! Fetch me my axe! I'll kill him! Even if I have to drag him to Niflheim myself,' growled King Ruffgar.

From under a damp bed of kelp, I witnessed how fierce and brave a warrior the Gutlander was. At Ruffgar's feet I saw the last of his loyal thanes dying before my eyes. Pawstein barked one last time at me:

'Beowuff! Lift me up to serve my Lord!'

But it was too late for Pawstein, he passed away from his wounds before I could fulfil his wish.

Besides, I was too busy concentrating on the matter of saving my own life.

'Beowuff! I will give you all my rings,' shouted Ruffgar, as I cowered under some kelp, 'and my collection of axes!' But what was the point of rings and axes if you are lying dead on a stony beach, waiting to be sliced into strips by the Hackerfolk?

'Sorry my Lord,' I whispered, safe under a pile of seaweed.

As soon as the coast was clear, I crawled out and took

to my heels. When I reached the first ridge, I climbed a dune to see how the battle was going. The wind was howling, so at first I didn't hear the voice behind me.

'Beowuff, what are you doing here? Do you have news of King Ruffgar?' asked Queen Ethelpelt.

'Erm, hello, my Queen. What brings you here?' I replied, not wanting to answer her questions.

'Is he victorious?' she asked.

'Not exactly, my Lady. The Hackerfolk are pretty vicious. They hack a lot,' I sighed.

'You can save him Beowuff,' she said firmly.

'Nothing can save him now, except magic,' I said

'I have magic,' she replied. 'Here!'

From under her mantle she produced a plain brown bag and handed it to me. 'You must do everything to save my Lord's life, Beowuff. I can trust you alone.'

Bench-mates, how I wish she hadn't put it like that!

'What is it?' I asked, but I already knew the answer.

I took the bag and felt the familiar shape. 'It will be an honour to look after this magic horn for you,' I said.

'When will you rejoin the battle?' she asked.

'Soon my Queen,' I said, 'but first I must fetch Ruffgar some help. Sailors, local peasants and the like. Fear not, for Muzzleguzzler will be completely safe with me.'

And with that I ran away from her and the battlefield as fast as I have ever run in my life.

If she called after me, her words were lost on the

wind as I fled with the magic horn safely in my loot-sack.

As I raced away I smiled and after a while I stopped to laugh and laugh and laugh. I had defeated Slainpile and escaped from the murderous Hackerfolk and come away without having to steal Muzzleguzzler – Queen Ethelpelt had actually given it to me herself!

I patted my deflated belly and for the first time since I landed on these dreary fish-eating flatlands I felt happy. I would have loved to have taken out the magic horn and examined it, but there was no time to waste.

Of course bench-mates, I had no intention of throwing away my life to help King Ruffgar.

As far as I could tell, there was little difference between the Lord of Gutland and the Hacker King. Both ruled with iron teeth and had their followers on short-leashes. Both held to a kind of warrior code. It is all very well to talk about 'fighting with honour' if you are as strong as an bear and you have a sword the size of a fjord. What in Gnor's name would be fair about a fight between me and the Hacker-King, or Slainpile, or any one of that pack?

Old Beowuffer has been a lie-sayer, a tale-teller, a loot-taker and sometimes even a death-mound-digger. I've been a brewer of troubles with an eye for the treasures of others. But is it not the Ruffgars and the Murderocs and their thug-dogs who have cast me in this mold?

Thieves and cheats do not normally go in for codes

but if we did, mine would go something like this:

> *'First for me and then for mine,*
> *Bodin take the pack behind.'*

King Ruffgar had dug his death-mound, and I would let him lie in it. I had to get out of Gutland alive and flee to safety with my treasure. So I tore down the beach, with Muzzleguzzler safe in my loot-sack. A little piece of advice from me bench-mates – always keep your loot-sack hidden under your tunic.

This was the scene: Hacker arrows were still turning the grey skies black. The air was thick with them and the few Gutlanders left standing looked to be carrying hedgehogs, not war-shields. Spears flew too, by the barge-load. All around me, I heard the howls of the wounded and the clash of metal on forged metal.

I was wondering how best to escape from this horror when I saw it – a flag sticking up over the rocks at the north end of the beach, twisting about in the wind. Attached to that yellow standard was the mast of Ruffgar's boat. I ran like a demon towards it.

In Gnor's name, the Swedish ship-builders had sold him a puppy for the price of a war-dog. It was a more flea-cutter than sea-cutter! The roaring dragon carved into its prow was undersized too, it looked like a wiggly worm.

I wondered whether the King's ship was guarded? Save for my show-down with Slainpile, your old hall-pal Beowuff had done neither biting nor fighting on this day and I was not about to start now.

Carefully, I began to creep towards the side of the shortship, till a terrible shriek hit my ears and sent me cowering onto the stones. A seagull took off and arced up into the sky.

I hid quietly behind a weed-wrapped rock and watched.

Presently, a figure came on deck. I could have praised the Bonefather and the rest of his godly pack, for it was none other than my old bench-mate Arnuf.

When I hailed him, he jumped up, barking for joy. Wagging his tail frantically, he bid me come aboard.

'Well met hall-pal!' I cried. 'What are you doing?'

'Guarding the ship,' said Arnuf sadly.

'How did we do? How is King Ruffgar?' he asked.

'He was living when I saw him last,' I answered, pleased with myself for telling a mistruth rather than an actual lie.

'How about Pawstein?'

I shook my head. Arnuf let out a howl.

'They got Pawstein! It's enough to make you weep, although he always used to bite me if I cried on duty.'

Alas for Arnuf! He was clearly gutted to have missed the fighting, whereas I would have gnawed off a hind leg to avoid it.

'Poor old Pawstein!' he moaned.

'Poor old Pawstein?' I cried. 'The beast who beat me around the hall? He almost ripped my ears off.'

'Aye, he had a decent bite on him,' sniffed Arnuf. 'Poor Pawstein, lovely lad, real shame,' he sighed.

I nodded, and was about to unleash my usual shower of drivel, when something stopped me. I decided that I could not let this stand.

'Arnuf,' I said. 'Think about this for a moment. Pawstein was the one who named you "leak-legged" and put you on death-mound duties. Pawstein pulled the feathers off that pigeon you thought was Longflapper's baby-hawk. Pawstein was the one who called you a bolt-battle and the name stuck. He even got the whole of Heorut hall playing the "Arnuf game".'

'What's the "Arnuf game?"' asked Arnuf. 'That sounds like fun. Can I play it?'

'Remember those two young pups outside the hall? Throwing buckets of water down each others legs and pretending to be leak-legged?' I sighed. 'That's the "Arnuf game" and you've got good old Pawstein to thank for it.'

'Pawstein was just having a laugh with the lads. "What goes on in the hall, stays in the hall" that's what he used to say.'

Although he was defending the brute, Arnuf's face fell and he lay down on the deck, downcast.

I'd meant to help him, but I fear that I had only reminded him of troubles that would have been better left forgotten.

'Here's a wise scrap of word-meat for you Arnuf,' I said. 'You're loyal alright, too loyal sometimes. So if I were you, I'd pick my bench-mates more carefully.'

And for once, I meant what I said.

Chapter thirteen

All I need is a short ship

As our shortship slipped its moorings, the Hackerfolk began to howl in celebration. It wasn't too hard to talk Arnuf into a 'rescue mission' to seek help for King Ruffgar. I was careful to breathe no word about the stolen horn, or my broken promises to the Queen.

My biggest worry now was that the Hackerfleet would spot us escaping and give chase. My heart began to beat faster as I spied row upon row of bladder-flying boats. I peered over the side at them and for a moment, I feared that the Hacker look-outs had raised the alarm.

Arnuf didn't seem worried, he pottered about the ship and got on with his duties.

'Lend a paw with this,' he called. I saw that he'd gripped a rope between his teeth and was hauling on it like a mad thing.

'Sorry Arnuf. Rope work is for sailors and we just agreed that I'm the Captain, remember?'

He panted, heaving harder.

'What in the name of Gnor are you doing?' I asked.

'Flying a flag,' he said.

'What flag?' I asked, dozing with the rocking motion of the waves.

'A pretty one with the golden crown on it.'

'Aaaaargh!' I screamed, leaping up in a panic. 'Get it down! Get it down now you weak-wit!'

'Why?' asked Arnuf. 'Don't you like flags?'

'That's Ruffgar's battle-standard!' I screamed.

'If the fleet sees that we've raised King Ruffgar's flag, we'll have every Hacker from here to Iceland on our tails! Get that accursed thing down before we are both hacked into caldron-sized pieces.'

Lowering Ruffgar's standard proved a lot harder than it should have been, as we were both in such a panic. When at last it was done, we lay staring at the lines of Hacker ships, squinting to see if any of them had broken ranks to come after us.

The Bonefather must have been smiling on us, for despite a few false alarms we managed to slip away unnoticed.

By the time the sun dipped into the sea, we had passed out of sight of the Hackerfleet. For the first time since that last night in Heorut hall, I felt hungry. So we feasted on biscuits and toasted our escape with a supply of meat-mead from a silver flask that I found in a sea-chest.

When morning came and the day unfolded, the sea looked flat, as if cast from a sheet of iron. The sun rose in the sky, but there was no wind to fill our sail.

'I like sailing,' said Arnuf, chewing a biscuit.

'This isn't sailing Arnuf. This is known as drifting. If only mighty Gnor would send us a firm breeze, to put some miles between us and Gutland.'

'Aren't we going back to Gutland?' whined Arnuf.

'Of course, but we need to put some distance between

us and the Hackers first,' I answered.

Arnuf fixed me with a stare for a moment and then trotted to the other end of the ship.

'What are you doing at the stern?' I asked.

He looked at me and tipped his head sideways.

'The back of the ship is called the stern Arnuf. Where that long pole thing is. That's called a rudder.'

'I'm looking for seagulls,' he answered.

A small wave rocked the ship, the sail billowed but fell slack once more. Arnuf sat gazing out into the distance, like a watchdog. Some time passed before I broke the silence.

'Alright Arnuf, you have my attention. Now why in the name of icy Nifelheim are you looking for seagulls?' I growled.

'To find out,' he muttered, lost in thought.

'To find out what?' I demanded.

'To find out why the seagulls follow the longship,' said Arnuf.

Before I had a chance to put an end to his nonsense, he spoke again, and this time it was a question that would have been laughable, were it not deadly serious.

'Are rudders and anchors the same thing?' he asked.

On hearing my simple command to "weigh the anchor" Arnuf had thrown away the long pole we were using to steer the ship. We had been drifting aimlessly all night until the current had brought us around in a circle, back into the jaws of the hated Hackerfleet.

Chapter Fourteen

Wolfe's Revenge

My heart was in my maw as I gazed in horror at the Hackerfleet. Even from this distance I could make out their loathsome blood-bladders waving in the wind. Sick with fear at this sight, I lay whimpering on the deck.

'Ships, ahoy! On the seaside,' cried Arnuf.

'On the "starboard side" Arnuf, not the "seaside".'

'And why in Gnor's name do you sound so pleased?'

'They're coming to rescue us,' said Arnuf. Then he started to shout loudly in the direction of the Hackers, 'Here! Here! We're over here!'

The half-wit was chasing around the deck, waving his paws frantically.

'Stop Arnuf! What are you doing?' I growled in a panic.

Suddenly, my bench-mate let out a frightened howl:

'Beowuff! I was wrong! It's the Hackerfleet! What in Gnor's name shall we do now?' he moaned.

'We'll ram them,' I cried. Then I realised we couldn't even steer, never mind get up enough speed to ram a warship. There was only one thing left to do.

'Arnuf, I have a plan,' I said. 'I'll jump overboard now. You stay here and hide.'

Then, I remembered the many times that the weak-wit had spoken up for me. Even old Beowuff wasn't heartless enough to leave him to be torn into strips for a Hacker's cook-pot.

I had run out of plans and plots. There was nothing left to do except stand and stare in silence.

One of the enemy ships broke away from the rest of the fleet and set a course for us.

Arnuf beat his tail frantically against the deck and began to bark the word 'Hack!'

'Arnuf, will you stop saying 'Hack!' as if you are a Hacker,' I growled.

The enemy ship was now upon us. However, there was something odd about it.

'Arnuf,' I began excitedly, 'what is the one thing that Hackerfolk carry with them wherever they go?'

'Hacking knives?' he offered.

'Well, yes, but what else?' I demanded.

'Er, cook pots? No! Blood-bladders on poles!' he barked in triumph.

'Exactly,' I said. 'But I can't see a single bladder on that ship, and I can't smell their cook-fire either.'

'That's a shame, I'm starved,' he moaned.

'Arnuf, the Hackers will be cooking the limbs of your dead bench-mates in their pots,' I sighed. 'But have no fear, for whoever may be on that ship, I doubt they can be as bad as the Hackerfolk.'

A wise Skald once said that 'hopes are often liars,' and so it proved in this case.

The ship was only yards away now and my joy turned to terror when a burly wolfhound with flashing eyes and rusty fangs bounded aboard.

'Beowuff!' he bayed. 'What enchantment is this?'

It was my old captor Captain Wolfe and he was mighty mad. He stuck his hairy muzzle right into my nostrils. 'A curse on ye, Beowuff. May Mac Lir flay your skull for what you did to me, you treacherous ditch-sniffer.'

Arnuf bounded over from the stern to join me.

'Who's your friend?' he asked.

'And who might ye be, ye little rat-sniffer?' asked the Irish Captain.

'I'm Arnuf of Gutland, Captain. It's a pleasure to meet a friend of Beowuff.'

Captain Wolfe lifted me by the throat and let out a howling laugh.

'Ohhh, yes! I am such a dear friend of this weasel. I have looked forward so much to seeing his handsome face again. Haven't I, Beowuff?' bellowed the Captain.

'It's great to have a ship-mate to share adventures with,' said Arnuf enthusiastically.

'Indeed it is. Just great,' growled the Captain, 'particularly when your 'ship-mate' tries to drown you by throwing chains round you. Aye! That's really 'great'. And then when he squeals like a kitten and he drags you down to hell and scrambles on your back to stop himself from drowning. That's 'great' too. Remember that, Beowuff?'

'I remember little of that dread night Captain,' I whimpered. 'But it won't happen again...'

'It won't, Beowuff. Have no fear. I'll make sure you suffer,' said Wolfe with a wicked grin.

'Captain, much has changed since we last met,' I said. 'There are things I could tell you that would be of great benefit to you.'

'Huh?' said Wolfe.

'Can we talk alone for a moment?' I whispered, pointing in the direction of Arnuf.

'You can talk alone all you like – when you're dangling in chains over the back of my longship!' howled Wolfe.

'Arnuf, can you go and see if there are any seagulls following our boat?' I asked.

'Aye,' said Arnuf. 'If I see one, shall I shoot it in the gullet?'

Arnuf trotted over to the stern, not seeming to notice the insults coming from the pack of weather-beaten faces on the pirate ship that was now lashed to ours.

'Listen Wolfe, things have changed since we last met. I am now famous in all of Gutland...'

'What are ye blabbing about?' laughed the Captain.

'I am best known for ridding King Ruffgar's hall of the Curse of Hendel and defeating King Murderoc's brother Slainpile in single combat,' I said.

'I have not heard of this,' growled the Captain.

'Been off a-viking again have you? Well you won't hear all the news when you're away plundering. But, as a reward for rescuing me, I would like to present you with one of the world's finest Skalds, given to me as a gift by Ruffgar, King of Gutland.'

'Where?' asked Wolfe, 'I don't see any Skalds aboard.'

'I don't want any gold for him Captain Wolfe,' I said pointing at Arnuf. 'You can take him as a present, a token of my appreciation for what you did for me in the great storm, which we have now forgotten.'

The wolfhound tilted his head one way and then the other.

'A Skald, you say? From Iceland?'

'They are the best. There just aren't enough of them to go round,' I answered.

'Bring him here,' he growled. I could see the rusty drool dripping from his iron fangs. 'But if this is another one of your Swedish tricks, you will regret every moment you spend alive.'

I nodded and called Arnuf back from the stern.

'Arnuf,' I said, 'I have great tidings for you.'

Wolfe barked an order to his crew and they threw over a huge leather collar which crashed onto the deck beside us.

'Arnuf, Captain Wolfe has agreed to rescue you. You need to go with him now. I have sorted it all out,' I called.

'What's that?' said Arnuf, pointing to the collar.

'It's a safety harness,' I said. 'His ship goes very fast across the water. It's great fun. I've done it many times. Put it on,' I smiled.

I wished it hadn't had to end this way but as the

poets say, 'each dog makes his own happiness'.

'No, Beowuff. I'm not going with him. You told me to choose my bench-mates more carefully.'

Arnuf was unshakeable as a terrier with its favourite stick.

'Now look Arnuf, the Hackerfolk are over there hacking everything in sight that belongs to Ruffgar.'

'The King won't stand for that. He's very particular about his things. Ruffgar rules with an iron claw, you know,' interrupted Arnuf.

'Well, yes, but I'll be amazed if he's got any claws left to rule with. The last time I saw him, everything was getting hacked off. Arnuf, you have to consider the other side – the good Captain Wolfe, whom I know well is offering to look after you in return for...' I said, trailing off.

'In return for what?' said Arnuf.

'In return for nothing, you curs,' barked Wolfe. 'He's no Skald.'

'Yes, he is!' I protested.

'No, I'm not,' said Arnuf.

'He's one of Iceland's finest,' I declared.

'I'm not a Skald from Icelandland! I'm a shore-guard from lower Gutland,' explained Arnuf.

Wolfe bared his rusty fangs and his hackles stood up like wires. I had to act now before the old rat-lasher tore my throat out.

'Captain, forget about the Skald,' I laughed. 'How do you like the sound of a golden treasure? Look!'

I produced the bag that held Muzzleguzzler from under my ripped cloak.

Slowly, I unwrapped the horn and Arnuf let out a flabbergasted whine.

'Muzzleguzzler! King Ruffgar's magic horn! Beowuff, how did you get that?'

For once I was glad of Arnuf's honesty.

Wolfe seized the treasure at once. Awe-stuck by its beauty and craftsmanship, he began to drool all over it.

'Let us toast this moment, Captain! Ruffgar's magic horn is yours. Let us drink!' I said.

'No! You go first,' said the wily Captain. Eyeing me suspiciously, he passed me the golden horn.

'No, Captain,' I said pushing the Muzzleguzzer back into his paws, 'we're drinking to your honour and it is only right that you sup from it first.'

The Captain was sorely tempted and put the horn to his lips, but he did not drink. Instead he gave it to Arnuf.

'Drink,' he laughed. 'Sup up Skald! For they don't have meat-mead where you are going.'

He let out a mad howl that set his pack baying.

As Arnuf took the Muzzleguzzler in his paws, my fickle heart was pounding. If Arnuf drank then the Captain would drink. Neither of them knew that by now I'd secretly slipped the packet of deadly Hensbane into the magic horn.

When the Captain supped, I would be rid of him for good! But, Captain Wolfe, curse his name, wouldn't drink a drop until Arnuf had tasted it first.

Well bench-mates, for the first time in all my days, I knew that I must make the right choice. I could not let poor Arnuf swig from that poisoned horn. He had harmed no one.

Alas, I'd made up my mind too late!

'Don't worry, Beowuff, I will save some for you,' said my shield-pal, raising the horn to his maw.

At that moment, from under my cloak came a secret voice that stopped him in his tracks.

The young fir that falls and rots
Has neither needles nor bark,
So is the fate of the friendless dog:
Why should he live long?

As he chanted these words, Rati the squirrel sprang out of nowhere and kicked away Muzzleguzzer before it touched Arnuf's lips. The golden treasure dropped to the deck with a clatter.

'What trickery is this?' brayed Wolfe. 'Who has conjured up this witch-spawn?'

Wolfe leapt at Rati but the squirrel was far too quick for the over-weight wolfhound and fled into the rigging. In his anger Wolfe belted Arnuf round the ear and snatched Muzzleguzzler up from the deck.

'Seize them!' he roared. At this command, the pack of sea-dogs swarmed onto our shortship and I was Wolfe's prisoner once again. Soon Arnuf and I were lashed to the mast of our undersized sea-cutter.

In his fury Wolfe sent two of his nimblest hounds to catch Rati but as the Sagas tell, you will never catch a squirrel without trickery or poison.

The chase went on for what seemed like an age until both hounds had lost their grip and crashed cursing into the sea. The sight of this sent Wolfe into a terrible rage. At last the crew urged the Captain to give up trying to catch Rati.

'Yeassh, Cap'n, ye'll have ye revenge soon enough,' howled a voice.

I shuddered. It was Bolt, my old gaoler, who had somehow escaped from drowning. The sound of his voice brought back grim memories of my time as a captive on board Wolfe's ship before I reached Gutland.

'Beowuff, you lying lick-spittle!' called the Captain from the highest deck. 'Hear the curse that I set upon you and your fake Skald and your prattling tree-rat. Now, all three of ye will taste Wolfe's revenge – and in Bodin's name I swear that I will savour it!'

With those words he was gone.

I was cold, hungry and very, very tired. I couldn't see Arnuf but I could hear him breathing.

'Arnuf?' I whispered.

'Yes?' he answered. 'Is there anything wrong Beowuff?'

'Arnuf! Of course there is. I have a bad feeling.'

'Well, it could be worse,' he said.

'How could it be any worse?' I asked in a fury. 'I

have lost my magic treasure and now I am tied to the mast of a rudderless shortship, in the hands of an insane Irish pirate bent on revenge against me. We are now condemned to drift to our doom or worse still, back into the midst of the Hackerfleet. How can it possibly be any worse than this?' I snapped.

'We could be dead,' said Arnuf.

'Well, that is a great comfort, Arnuf. Only death would be worse than this. I feel so much better,' I said.

'If you feel better, I feel better,' he replied.

It all went very quiet again. I felt the boat rocking uneasily but I couldn't see a thing because that accursed sea-pack had lashed my muzzle to the mast.

'Arnuf? Where are Captain Wolfe and his crew? Can you see what they are doing?' I croaked, choking on my collar as I tried to get my words out.

'Fear not bench-mate,' he answered. 'They've gone back onto their own boat. 'Oh look! They are all waving goodbye. Pity I can't wave back – my paws are tied to the mast. Look! They're laughing and pointing. I wonder what our gift is?'

'Gift? What gift?' I barked in a panic. 'Arnuf? Can you smell smoke? What's happening?' I screamed in terror but the weak-wit wasn't paying attention.

'Ah-ha!' he cried. 'I know what the present is – the one they threw over to us just now. It's an oil lamp.'

'Arnuf!!!!!!!!!!!!!!!!!!!!!!' I screamed...

From the mast above came a familiar voice.

Brand kindles brand till they burn out.

135

Fire is quickened by fire.
It is best for a dog to be middle-wise,
Not over cunning and clever.

'Rati?' I cried, as the billowing smoke clogged my lungs. 'Rati is that you?'

'Aye, the very same,' laughed the squirrel climbing down the mast until we were nose to nose.

'Rati! I have a favour to beg of you,' I cried.

'Choose your words carefully Beowuff, for my master is not best pleased with how you have behaved.'

'King Ruffgar?' I coughed, 'Surely he's not still alive?'

Rati let out a chattering laugh.

'Ruffgar is not my master, as you may find out one day. But ask quickly, for my tail grows hot.'

'With pleasure!' I answered. 'Please oh true-hearted tree-squirrel, can you save your old...'

'Ah ah ha!' interrupted the squirrel. 'Ask wisely Beowuff. Choose your words with care, or they'll be the last ones you speak in this world or the next.'

I let out a howl of disbelief. Here I was, tied to the mast of a burning shortship, and the only chance of rescue came from a talking squirrel who wanted me to watch my mouth.

The ship's timbers cracked as the fire took hold. The wooden deck began to steam and hiss with the power of the flames, which were now spreading to the mast. I let out a little whine of despair.

I racked my smoke-scorched brain to think of what I

should say to answer the squirrel. Through the shrouds of smoke, my eyes settled on the face of my weak-witted bench-mate.

'Middle-wise,' I muttered, 'that would be a big improvement for Arnuf.'

'Hurry!' called Rati, 'For my paws grow hotter!'

All of a sudden, it came to me. I knew with full certainty what I had to say.

'Oh kind-hearted squirrel! Please can you save US?' I begged.

'Well said!' laughed the creature and he leapt down onto the deck and then shot away into the hold faster than one of Gnor's lightening bolts.

'Curse you! You false-mouthed tree-rat,' I screamed, shaking a furious paw in his direction. 'You promised to help me if I asked wisely!'

At that moment, I realised that my paws were free. The ropes that Wolfe's pack had lashed me to the mast with had been nibbled clean through by unearthly teeth.

The boat pitched suddenly as the burning rail gave way and fell crashing into the sea. We were now sinking fast and it was time to abandon our shortship before it abandoned us.

'Arnuf!' I cried. 'What in the name of the Bearded Bonefather do you think you are doing?'

'Nosing about,' he replied. 'Mmmm! I think I can smell kippers in here.'

I saw that he had his nose in a large barrel that had

suddenly appeared out of the smoke-murk.

'Make haste you dawdling fish-sniffer!' I called, pushing him out of the way and climbing into the cask. 'Pull your silly snout out of there and get rolling. When I'm safely inside you can shove me over the stern. If this thing holds water I could float my way back to Gutland.'

Arnuf twisted his head to the side and looked at me with those sad brown eyes and let out a puzzled whine.

'On second thoughts, you get in,' I sighed, changing places with him. 'I'd better do the rolling.'

'Whatever you say bench-mate,' he laughed.

BEOWUFF
AND THE
Dragon
Raiders

Viking dog Beowuff is all bark and no bite, a disgrace to the memory of his fierce ancestors.
Beowuff turns tail and flees from Hendel and the Hackers, only to find himself snatched by a scurvy pack of bone raiders. Mange is the least of his worries when he learns about the fiery fate that awaits him and his weak-witted side-kick Arnuf on Dragongeld island.

ISBN: 9781906132392
UK £7.99 USA $14.95/ CAN $16.95

Some of Beowuff's adventures might sound familiar to history lovers, because they echo the ancient tale of Beowulf (1000 A.D.), one of the earliest recorded poems in Old English.

"My husband, professor Burns-Longship has made a second incredible find! This time there are dragons involved as well as Viking dogs! Surely now the experts in Scandinavia will return my calls!"
– Mrs Burns-Longship, The Village Blog.

I AM SPARTAPUSS

By Robin Price

In the first adventure in the Spartapuss series...
Rome AD 36. The mighty Feline Empire rules the world.
Spartapuss, a ginger cat is comfortable managing Rome's
finest Bath and Spa. But Fortune has other plans for him.
Spartapuss is arrested and imprisoned by Catligula, the
Emperor's heir. Sent to a school for gladiators, he must fight
and win his freedom in the Arena – before his opponents
make dog food out of him.

'This witty Roman romp is history with cattitude.'
Junior Magazine (Scholastic)

ISBN 13: 978-0-9546576-0-4
UK £7.99
USA $14.95/ CAN $16.95

The Spartapuss Series:

I Am Spartapuss (Book I)
Catligula (Book II)
Die Clawdius (Book III)
Boudicat (Book IV)
Cleocatra's Kushion (Book V)

www.mogzilla.co.uk

CATLIGULA

By Robin Price

'Was this the most unkindest kit of all?'

In the second adventure in the Spartapuss series...

Catligula becomes Emperor and his madness brings Rome to within a whisker of disaster. When Spartapuss gets a job at the Imperial Palace, Catligula wants him as his new best friend. The Spraetorian Guard hatch a plot to destroy this power-crazed puss in an Arena ambush. Will Spartapuss go through with it, or will our six-clawed hero become history?

ISBN 978-0-9546576-1-1
UK £6.99
USA $10.95/ CAN $14.95

DIE CLAWDIUS

By Robin Price

'You will die, Clawdius!'

In third adventure in the Spartapuss series...

Clawdius, the least likely Emperor in Roman history, needs
to show his enemies who's boss. So he decides to invade
Spartapuss' home – The Land of the Kitons.
As battle lines are drawn, Spartapuss must take sides.
Can the magic of the Mewids help him to make the right
choice?

*'Another fantastic story in this brilliantly inventive series.
Any reader (young and old) will enjoy these books!'*
Teaching and Learning Magazine

ISBN 978-095-46576-8-0
UK £6.99   USA $10.95/ CAN $14.95

In the first *London Deep* adventure...

Jemima Mallard is having a bad day. First she loses her air, then someone steals her houseboat, and now the Youth Cops think she's mixed up with a criminal called Father Thames. Not even her dad, a Chief Inspector with the 'Dult Police, can help her out this time. Oh – and London's still sinking. It's been underwater ever since the climate upgrade.

ISBN: 978-1-906132-03-3 £7.99

www.mogzilla.co.uk/londondeep

Chosen as a 'Recommended Read' for World Book Day 2011.
One of the *Manchester Book Award's* 24 recommended titles for. 2010.

MOGZILLA

ABOUT THE TRANSLATOR

Professor Burns-Longship speaks five languages (three of them 'dead' and one on its last legs). Despite his widely reported spat with Dr Sven Smugaxe of the Stockholm Institute of Vikingology, Professor Burns-Longship is still generally acknowledged to be the world's leading authority on Viking dogs. He lives and works in the charming village of Wuffton-Basset, although his field-trips take him everywhere from Oxford to Oslo. When not translating Beowuff sagas, he writes for *The Village Blog*.